Two Sisters
A STORY OF FREEDOM

To my mother, Makeda, and all the sacrifices you made.

While the events described and some of the characters in this book may be based on actual historical events and real people, the characters created by the author are fictional and their stories a work of fiction.

Published in the UK by Scholastic Children's Books, 2021
Euston House, 24 Eversholt Street, London NW1 1DB, UK
A division of Scholastic Ltd

London ~ New York ~ Toronto ~ Sydney ~ Auckland
Mexico City ~ New Delhi ~ Hong Kong

Text © Kereen Getten, 2021
Cover illustration © Alette Straathof, 2021

ISBN 978 0702 30184 1

Printed and bound by CPI Group (UK) Ltd, Croydon, CR0 4YY

2 4 6 8 10 9 7 5 3 1

The right of Kereen Getten to be identified as the author of this work respectively has been asserted by them in accordance with the Copyright, Designs and Patents Act, 1988.

www.scholastic.co.uk

Two Sisters
A STORY OF FREEDOM

KEREEN GETTEN

Series Consultant:
Tony Bradman

■SCHOLASTIC

1.

RUTH

Falmouth, Jamaica
1781

I raced through the plantation of River House, my dress kicking out in front of me, dashing through rows of sugar cane. I weaved through the tall grass-like clumps, laughter caught between short breaths, trying to distance myself from my half-sister, Anna, who was closing in.

If she caught me, my punishment would be to serve Mistress Charity, the white lady who came to the house at least once a week to bother Master John Ambrose, the plantation owner. Mistress Charity was desperate to be Master John's second wife. His first wife died some years ago, long before Anna was born, but Master John was never interested in remarrying, so he would force Anna to entertain Mistress Charity while he locked himself in his study, pretending to be busy.

Anna didn't like entertaining Mistress Charity, who was wicked with a short temper and a quick hand. So, she had challenged me to a race – whoever lost would have to do the other's chores for an entire week. That included scrubbing the floors, changing bedpans, beating the rugs and, most importantly, dealing with Mistress Charity.

Anna must have thought it would be an easy win, which is why she had suggested the game. I laughed at the idea that my younger sister could catch me.

"Look at your dress," I told her. "You will trip over that hem within two seconds."

She smirked, her light brown eyes glistening, "Then you won't be afraid of a little bet."

We spat on our palms and shook hands to seal the deal. Then Anna turned her back, covered her eyes and counted from one to ten. This gave me enough time to slip off my shoes before clearing the steps of the porch and running towards the fields.

I wasn't wrong about Anna struggling. She dressed like a white lady with too much money and not enough to do. The sort that paced their veranda fanning themselves violently because they were too hot, but still wanted to wear those ridiculous dresses.

As well as owning the plantation, Master John was also Anna's father, and he often brought back pretty – but inconvenient – dresses from England for her. They always had frills that crawled up Anna's neck, puffy long sleeves that itched her skin, and a ridiculous number of bows on the front – all beautiful to look at, but far too hot for the Jamaican sun.

Anna would try to share these with me, but I was much taller than her and besides, I would rather not be weighed down by unnecessarily extravagant outfits.

I hid behind a tall stalk about six feet high to catch my breath. I had reached the path in the middle of the plantation that separated one side from the other. It was where the overseer rode his horse on the dirt road watching over everyone as they slaved under the heat with little rest.

To get to the other side, I had to cross the road without the overseer, Walter, spotting me. He was evil. Worse than the manager of the sugar-cane mill or the clerks that helped him with his duties.

It was obvious from when I was old enough to understand that Walter had a great dislike for me and Anna, but more so me. It was also common knowledge on the plantation that he happened to be Master John's cousin.

Walter was the main overseer on the plantation. Nothing happened without his say-so. He was a rough-looking man with a constant scowl under his moustache, dark evil eyes hidden under his broad-brimmed hat, and a deep scar on his left cheek from when a slave defended himself during a beating.

The slave paid with his life.

Walter never went anywhere without that hat. Sometimes, I daydreamed about stealing it while he slept and filling it with biting ants.

Mama said it was because he despised the special treatment we received from Master John. When Anna was four years old, her father allowed Mama and me into the house. It was more convenient, he said; Mama could get up in the night with Anna and he wouldn't have to send for her.

Anna had a bedroom on the same floor as his, while Mama and me he allowed a back room on the ground floor. Mama became the housemistress, which didn't go down well with many, but especially angered Walter.

Up until then, Walter had been given free rein around the plantation. Master John was often too busy with the accounting or travelling to England, so he never questioned Walter's decisions. Until things changed with Mama.

"I will not interfere with how you conduct your business," Master John had told him the day we moved in to the house. "But you will not touch Liza or her child, and you will most certainly not touch Anna."

Walter did not take kindly to those rules. In fact, it made him worse.

He accused me of stealing sugar cane and eating it. He bribed one of the house girls to plant a china cup under Mama's bed. He hadn't dared try anything with Anna yet; he knew if he overstepped, Master John would have to get rid of him. Still, to him, we were all the same – even if Anna's skin was as pale as moonlight. We were all slaves. In fact, he was the only one who treated her like one of us. The only person who saw us standing side by side – Anna with her fair skin and light hair, me with my dark skin and braids – and looked at *both* of us with disgust.

The worst thing he did was try to sell me one time when Master John was away in England on business. Walter went on a rampage looking for us, but Cook hid us inside the fireplace, covering us with wood, and everyone protected us. Even as they were whipped, one by one, no one gave us up.

Walter wasn't someone to be trifled with. Especially being so far away from the house and out of Master John's earshot. But I was never one to let a small matter of an overseer who wanted me gone get in the way of having fun. It was the one thing about me that drove Mama mad, and the thing Anna and I constantly fought about.

"Ruth, wen yaah gonna learn dat man looking fi a reason tuh sell yuh?" Mama would say after saving me from Walter's grasp for the hundredth time.

"What should I do?" I had asked. "Lock mi self in di house and never leave?"

Mother shot me a cutting look. She had made me learn 'proper English' alongside Anna, whom Master John insisted on having lessons, and would scold me whenever I slipped into Jamaican Patois. The two were similar and yet completely different; the Patois rolled off my tongue like a song, where the English felt stiff and sharp.

"Yes," Mama had replied with Cook echoing her, "Dat exactly wah yuh muss do if dat wah it takes."

But that wasn't what I wanted. I loved the outdoors. I spent so much time cleaning floors, making beds and emptying bedpans that the sun always called me outside.

The swaying leaves from the sugar cane whispered to me, begging me to come out and play. I could not ignore it. Even if Walter stood on the steps with a whip in his hand, I would find a way to feel the wind on my face. It was the only time I felt free, even at the risk of having my freedom taken away.

I peeked through the leaves, looked left, down the

long dirt road, then right. There he was, about thirty feet away from me, climbing off his horse, the thick black whip hanging loosely off the hook of his trousers. Betty, he called that whip. Betty, his best friend.

I tiptoed out of the grass and stepped on to the road with just the tip of my toes, as though the dirt road would tell on me if it felt my soles.

I heard a movement behind and peered over my shoulder only to see Anna creeping towards me gleefully. I covered my mouth to hide the squeal, and dashed across the road, diving into the grass on the other side.

The grass was thicker this side of the plantation. The slaves had not started cutting down this side of the road yet. It was easier to hide here; the cane leaves towered over me at least twelve feet high. I pushed my way through, keeping close to the road. Anna was closing in on me, much to my surprise. She didn't seem to have stopped once, but when I took a quick glance over my shoulder, her hair was frizzled from the heat, and I thought how angry Mama would be when she saw her so dishevelled and unladylike.

I felt a pang of guilt for my sister. Anna was, after all, the reason why I was not slaving away in the fields the way the overseer would like.

It was because of Anna that I was allowed inside the

big house. Mama said if she had not had Anna, who knows what would have happened to us. Just like Papa was sold to someone else, the same thing could have happened to us.

I couldn't remember Papa. Mama said it was because I was only a babe when he was taken from us. She rarely spoke about him and when she did, her face would go blank and she would get this wild, terrified look in her eyes. So, I stopped mentioning him.

Anna was our saviour. The more I thought about all the attention and special treatment she got, the angrier I became, and I was about to call off the game when a familiar sound stopped me dead in my tracks.

I listened carefully, heart dropping to my feet. There it was again. A sound I had heard too often; the same sound that woke me in the middle of the night, sweating and gasping for breath.

I squinted through the tall grass and spied the overseer testing his whip against the ground. The swish it made through the air sent chills through me. It was a thing he did before you felt the whip on your skin. It was meant to unnerve you, set you on edge, not knowing when the blow would fall. I leaned further out to get a better look. Behind the shadow of the overseer, there was a young girl tied to a tree, her hands bound behind her.

I knew that girl. I knew everyone, but this particular girl, Sarah, was born the same day as me. We were birthday twins. Her mama and mine were bought together. When we moved into the house Mama got Sarah a job in the kitchen, so I didn't understand why she was out here, tied to a tree, about to be whipped. I pushed through the thick stalks frantically, my breathing so loud anyone around me could have heard it. This is when Mama would have told me to mind my business, to let grown people handle it. I reached the last row of leaves that hid me and lowered myself to the ground.

The overseer was just a few feet away. He was so close I could smell him. He smelt of tobacco and sweat, and a stench adults describe as death. He smelt of death.

I took a deep breath and stepped out into the open.

2.

ANNA

I saw what she was about to do and raced through the long grass, grabbing her just as she stepped out into the open.

"Ruth, no," I hissed. She tried to pull her dress out of my firm grip. But I held on for dear life.

"Please," I begged. "It's not your concern."

"But it is," Ruth argued. She tried to leave again but I yanked her back, knowing it was exactly what Mama would do if she were here.

"Ruth, *please.*" My voice broke as I tried to get her to understand. We weren't really supposed to be out here; Mama said it was too dangerous, and she was right. I would happily have played inside all day, but not Ruth. There was a certain defiance about her. She wouldn't be told what to do. She was fearless and her fearlessness got her into trouble.

She was angry at me. I could see it in her face, the way her eyebrows pushed together making lines in her forehead.

"Yuh might be able to turn yuh eyes away, Anna, as though di sun is blinding yuh," Ruth hissed. "But," she pointed towards the girl, "dat could be mi, and one day, it will be. What will yuh do then? Say it is not yuh concern?"

My face fell that she could ever think such a thing.

"That isn't fair, and you know it."

The sound of the whip on the ground made us both jump and I was ready to leave, but I could see in her eyes she was not.

"Don't stop me, Anna, or I will never speak to yuh again. Yuh hear?" She turned on her heels and ran out into the road just as the overseer raised the whip above his head.

Heart pounding so loud it was thick in my ears, I ran back the way I had come. Through the long grass, across the road, into the banana trees. I ran as fast as I could but it didn't seem fast enough. The dress was holding me back, so I stopped and stripped off the layers of petticoats and threw them to the side. I paused, before picking up each petticoat, folding them neatly and carrying them under my arm. My chest ached but I no longer heard the whip and that only made me run faster. I reached the house and ran around the side, bumping into Alfred, one of the clerks.

"Watch it, girl," he snapped. I apologized profusely, running around him and towards the kitchen, where I could hear Mama singing. The kitchen was separate from the house, a building on its own, and the doors were open, with the smell of sweet porridge filling the air. Outside the kitchen I looked for somewhere to hide the petticoats from Mama. I found a stone behind the door and stored them under it for later.

I took a deep breath and ran in and yelled, "Mama," loud enough for her to hear but not too loud that it would be unladylike. The singing stopped, and she and the other ladies turned to look at me.

Mama's face fell. "Anna! Why yuh look like dat? Ruth tek you to di fields again?"

She started her usual telling-off about how it was not ladylike, that I wasn't to follow my sister because now I looked improper, like someone who didn't have a home.

She marched over to me, licked her thumb and pressed my hair down, all the while talking. I cringed under the feel of her spit on my skin and she told me to stop moving; that I did this to myself. Joshua, one of the field boys, appeared in the doorway, out of breath.

"Mistress Liza," he said. "Come quick. Di overseer 'ave Ruth."

Mama stopped what she was doing, lifted her dress above her knees and started to run. I didn't have time to tell her that was why I was there. Mama ran through the back of the house and I ran around it, to the front door where I knew she would appear. I didn't go in with her because I didn't want Papa to see me. I didn't want him to know I had been in the fields.

I waited at the bottom of the steps, pacing, biting my nails – a bad habit I picked up from when I was a baby. Joshua waited behind me not saying a word. Eventually, I turned and he was looking at me strangely.

"I was going to tell her about Ruth," I mumbled.

He nodded.

"Yes, miss."

I turned away from him, glancing up at the door, which was still closed.

I turned back, biting my nails. "She didn't give me time, that's all."

He nodded again, agreeable but not agreeing. I didn't have the same sort of relationship with everyone that Ruth did. I didn't spend any time outside the house if I could help it, not unless Ruth dragged me to one of the parties held by the workers' houses. Being among the slaves made me feel a guilt I still could not describe. I felt their eyes on me, judging, wondering what I was doing among them in my silk dress and bows. I was more aware of myself when I was with them.

Suddenly, the door opened and Papa marched out not looking too pleased, Mama running beside him.

"I can't keep interfering in field business," he was saying, barely touching the steps. As he reached me, he glanced in my direction. He took me in: my unkempt hair, my dress marked by passing branches and dirt from the ground.

He sighed. "Can't you keep her clean?" he said to Mama before heading towards the plantation.

When they reached the dirt road, I ran into the fields to hide, afraid that Ruth would think I interfered. I stumbled through the tall leaves, all the while keeping an eye on Mama and Papa, who approached the crowd now forming. Papa pushed through the crowd just as the overseer raised his whip above his head, and through the parted crowd I saw Ruth standing in front of Sarah, blocking her from the whip.

"Stop this at once!" Papa shouted, marching towards them with Mama beside him. I let out a trembling breath of relief when the overseer lowered his whip.

My father was usually a quiet man. He didn't raise his voice, even when he was angry. But his face would get tight and he would stare for so long it made people feel small. He marched up to the overseer, who lowered the whip, so it hung on the ground swinging from side to side, still menacing, still hoping.

"You were specifically told not to lay a hand on that girl," Papa said, stopping just a few steps from the overseer as they met each other eye to eye.

"She is a slave," he spat. "One who was interfering in business that did not concern her," Walter replied, matter of fact.

Papa stepped closer. "You will stand down," he said in a low but steady voice. "Or you will lose your job."

For a moment it seemed like the overseer was not going to move, but then he did; he stepped back.

Mama rushed over to untie Sarah's arms from the tree. She whispered something to her, and Sarah ran towards the house. She then turned to Ruth, checking her face for any marks, moving Ruth's face from side to side as she looked her over.

When she realized she was unharmed, Mama dragged her away by her arm. I hurried after them, catching up as they headed back to the house.

"Why you keep putting yourself in danger like dis,

Ruth?" Mama said, her tone lowered so that only we could hear.

"What else am I to do?" Ruth cried, trying to keep up with her mother without stumbling.

"*Walk away,*" her mother snapped. "It is her or you. You understand dat? We can't save everybody."

Papa caught up with us after exchanging a few heated words with Walter, and the three of us headed back to the house. We avoided going through the sugar cane and followed the dirt road that twisted through the plantation and up towards the house. I tried to take Ruth's hand but she pulled away.

"Where did you go?" she asked.

I twisted my fingers in front of me, lowering my head. "You told me you would never speak to me again if I stopped you. I didn't know what to do so I hid."

Ruth glared at me angrily. "You did not call your papa?"

I bit the inside of my lip, tears clouding my vision. Ruth shook her head and ran to catch up with Papa and Mama. I wanted to tell her that I had tried, but what use would it be when she wouldn't believe me. I followed behind at a distance.

"You have to get rid of him," Mama said, running to keep up with Papa's long strides. "He will kill her."

Papa shook his head, "Not many men will accept

the pay I am offering for the job." He glanced over at Mama regretfully. "And he is family."

I had heard rumours of Walter being Papa's cousin, but it was just too horrible to consider that he and I could be *related*.

We walked through the large gardens of River House Sugar Plantation, set in the hills of Falmouth, Jamaica. In the distance was the two-storey house, perched on a slight elevation, with wrap-around balconies on both floors, and steps with white railings leading to the veranda. The lower part of the house was made of stone, while the upper part was made of white wood.

River House was the only plantation for miles. It had a long sweeping road that led in and out of the property but Ruth and I had never seen the end of it. We had never left the plantation, although I once overheard Papa say the land was over a thousand acres, which I repeated to Ruth because Ruth loved to know what was outside those walls. Neither of us could imagine what a thousand acres looked like but thought it might be the whole island.

Six buildings surrounded the main house. The kitchen, a long stone building to the right of the house; a separate office a little way to the left by the coconut tree; a boiling house and a sugar factory closer to the fields, with a carriage house and a coach house further down the hill. A mile north of the fields was a river that ran through the hills. Sometimes we joined the women on the trail to collect water.

Mama and Papa entered the house through white doors already open and moved along the dark wooden floor. Mama continued to plead with him but as they reached his office on the right, he stopped and turned.

"Enough, Liza," he said sharply. "Just mind her more. Stop her from running off. Give her something to do." He entered the office, closing the door behind him. Mama stared at the closed door, then at us. There was a pain in her eyes, the kind of pain that looks helpless.

"Get to work," she said to us quietly before heading down the hall and out of the back door.

I reached for Ruth's fingers and tried to link hers with mine. "I'm sorry I didn't stay with you," I told her through watery eyes. "Please don't be angry with me."

Ruth sighed. "All you had to do was get your papa."

I felt the warm tears fall. "I'm sorry. I am not as brave as you, Ruth. I tried. I promise I did." Ruth opened her mouth to say something but she was interrupted by the sound of hooves coming towards us. Walter the overseer rode up to the veranda, pulling the horse to a stop at the bottom of the steps.

He loomed over us from his saddle, his mouth pulled up into an unsettling smile.

"One day, he won't be here to save you," he said, "then I'll have you both sent to the slave market. You will fetch a good price." He looked at me. "Especially you."

I inhaled sharply. Ruth reached across to steady me.

"Can he do that?" I whispered, horrified. "Can he sell me?" I always knew Ruth and Mama were at risk of being taken away, that I was the one who kept them here, but if I could be sold, who would save them? Who would save me?

Ruth tightened her hand around mine and she squeezed it tightly. "He won't hurt you," she said with a quiet anger. "I won't let him."

3.

RUTH

I took my shaken sister upstairs to her bedroom, across the hall from her father's room. There were seven rooms in total along the long hall with its yellow walls and wood floor. But only the two bedrooms were ever used.

Anna's room was large, with a balcony overlooking the plantation as far as the eye could see. White wooden shutters kept the light out in the day, and the insects out at night. Although her father liked to spoil her, inside the room was nothing much to look at except a dark mahogany four-poster bed that sat in the middle of the room facing the door, a dresser and a wardrobe against the opposite wall. The walls were covered in a pattern of green flowers to match the bed sheets and the curtains pulled back against the bedposts.

I opened the wardrobe, searching for a dress that would distract her from Walter's threats even though I was just as afraid as her. I decided on a pale blue dress with long sleeves, a high collar and dark stripes.

I threw the dress at her with a small bow, "Mi lady."

Anna caught it with a watery smile. When she was dressed, she sat at the vanity mirror while I fitted a small brown hat with a blue feather over her hair.

When I finished dressing her, I took her hand and we paraded down the stairs as if we were ladies with an audience waiting at the foot of the stairs. We nodded and smiled to our invisible crowd. I led her by the hand into the front drawing room, one of four on the lower floor, and the largest.

The dark wooden floor that was the same throughout the house was covered only by a few small tables and the odd chair against a painted wall. Folding shutter doors that matched the windows opened up on to a wide veranda, which allowed a welcome breeze in the evening.

We spent the afternoon making up clapping games, pretending to be rich white ladies, then we sneaked Sarah and Cook's six-year-old son, William, out of the kitchen to play Switch. For the game, one person would take a thin branch that resembled the overseer's whip and hide it. Everybody had to find the hidden switch and the first one to find it got to whip the others.

Normally we played it outside, but after what happened that day, none of us wanted to risk it. Sarah told William to run outside and find a stick to play with. He was the smallest, and less likely to get a hiding.

"Mi nuh want to," he whined, folding his short arms against his chest.

"Yuh have tuh," Sarah told him, pushing him out the back door. He tried to get back in but Sarah blocked his way.

"He nah hurt yuh," Sarah tried to convince him. "He nuh hurt small children." But we all knew that was a lie. Walter never did discriminate on age; it was whoever was in his way.

"Dat nuh true," William argued, "him try hurt mi many times."

I nudged Sarah out of the way and stepped outside to show William there was nothing to be afraid of, even though the hairs on my neck were standing up. I reached for his hand.

"Come, William," I said. "I will look with you."

"Ruth," Anna said anxiously, and I knew what she was thinking but I ignored her, swinging William's arm playfully so he wouldn't be afraid. I scanned outside the kitchen for Walter, but I couldn't see or hear him.

Only Cook was singing.

"What did you do today?" I asked him cheerily.

William kicked a stone in front of him, "Mi put the grass into a pile after they cut the cane down an' cleaned up but mi wasn't fast enough, so the bad man got angry." I nodded as if listening but my eyes scanned the ground quickly. At the edge of the field I picked the first stick I saw, relieved we didn't have to go any further.

"This will do," I said, showing it to a nervous William. "Race you back to the house!"

William didn't need to be told twice. He raced to the back door, pushing past the girls, almost falling inside.

Inside we let him hide the whip while we covered our faces. When he had hidden it, he called us excitedly.

"Ready, ready, ready," he said, jumping up and down.

We separated. I headed for the office even though William knew not to go in there. I was about to go in when I heard voices inside.

I pressed my ear against the door and listened. Inside, I heard Mama pleading with Master John to take us to England on his next visit.

"They will be safe there," she begged him.

"And how will I explain their presence?" Master John asked. "What do I tell my family when I bring them to their door?"

There was a pause as if Mama was stunned, and when she spoke it was clear that she was. "You tell them they are yours," she said, as though baffled the question was even being asked.

"*Anna* is mine," Master John corrected her in a lowered voice. "And even she will have trouble. What will I do with Ruth? Hmm? What will I do with her?"

I turned on my heels and ran down the hall and into the library. I found a corner and huddled as far against the wall as I could, knees pressed into my chest.

That was where Anna found me a while later. On the floor, squeezed between two bookcases. Anna sat down next to me and asked what was wrong. I explained to her everything I had heard.

"He's taking you to England," I mumbled into my dress. "You will get to wear pretty dresses every day, and attend parties, and there will be no Walter, or whips or threats to sell you. You will be free, Anna, just like Mama said you would."

Anna wrapped her arms around my back and rested her head on mine. "I won't go anywhere without you, Ruth," she whispered, "I promise." She climbed to her feet and disappeared around the corner. She returned minutes later with a book in her hand. It was one of our favourites, *Goody Two Shoes*.

A few years ago, Master John had made sure that

Anna learned to read and write. She had struggled at first and Mama had insisted I sit with her while she practised, even though I didn't know how to read or write either.

Still, I would sit with her and get her to show me, slowly.

Repeating what she had learned each day helped her learn faster and I picked up a few things too. I couldn't read nearly as well as her, and I couldn't really write much, but it was enough.

Master John had brought the book back from England as a present for Anna once she had finished her lessons. At first I was jealous, but Anna had shared it and together we took turns reading it.

Anna opened the book, turning to the first page. They were a little worn from all the times we had read it. She began to read in a low tone, her voice soothing as it always was when Anna read. She had this quietness about her that could often be frustrating, but right then, in the corner of the library, our dresses hitched above our knees, it was soothing to listen to.

As Anna read, I lifted my head and leaned against the bookcase. It was hard to focus on reading when all I could think about was Anna leaving.

It was still dark outside when Mama woke us.

Anna had sneaked into my bed, afraid the overseer might come for us in the night. We had wrapped our arms around each other tightly so if he tried to take one, he would have to take us both.

I woke to a hard shake. My first thought was that the overseer had come to get me, so when I opened my eyes I expected to see him standing over me.

But what looked back at me was Mama's fearful eyes urging me to get up and get dressed. Before my eyes could adjust to the dark room, Mama had already rushed around to the other side of the bed to wake Anna.

"Get dressed," she said, handing us our dresses, "quickly."

I climbed out of bed, confused, and slipped into my clothes.

"Mama," I said, trying to catch her attention as she scurried around the room. "What's happening?"

Mama ignored my question, pulling our coats on, and then the hats we rarely wore, securing them with a ribbon. I glanced at the window and it was pitch black outside. She paused for a second when she was done and looked at us with tears in her eyes.

She forced a smile before turning away.

"Come," she said, opening the door, "and no mek

no noise." She threw a glance at me and I nodded obediently, too scared to be offended. We followed her along the hall, down the stairs and towards the front of the house.

The front door was open and a carriage was waiting outside. Anna's hand tightened around mine. Outside the carriage, Master John was waiting, dressed in his long black coat and top hat. He exchanged a few words with Liza and they both turned to look at us.

Mama beckoned us forward. She placed a hand on our cheeks, choking back tears.

"Mi girls." She looked at Anna, "Esi," she said, and then she turned to me. "Ami."

We were forbidden from using our Ashanti given names, so we kept it a secret and only used it between us.

"Mi loves, Master John will take you both to England. Yuh will be safe deh; him will make sure of it."

I stared at Mama, confused. "Me an' Anna?"

Mama nodded, stroking my face.

"Yuh mus speak English over deh. Dey won't understand yuh, yuh hear?"

I nodded. "You comin' too, Mama?"

She shook her head smiling, "No, Ami, but yuh will see mi again soon, mi promise."

"But you will visit?" Anna asked.

Mama quickly glanced at Master John. She wavered,

"Yes," as she kissed us both on the forehead. "Mi soon come. Now, hurry, get in."

I climbed into the carriage after Anna and Master John followed, closing the door. Mama leaned in through the window, tears streaming down her face. "Be good," she said. "Anna, look after your sister; she will need you." She turned to me. "Ruth, please, yuh must do as dem tell you, or dem will send you back, and mi can't protect yuh if yuh come back." She pulled me towards her and whispered, "It wasn't easy getting you on the boat, Ruth. Don't ruin it."

I nodded, placing my hand over my mother's.

"I promise, Mama," I said through tears, "I'll be good."

The carriage started to move and I gripped on to her hand for dear life, forcing her to run alongside until finally she let go, blowing us kisses. I leaned out of the window as the carriage made its way along the road leading out of the plantation; my last glimpse was of her crumbling to the ground.

4.

RUTH

The journey to England was long. We spent the first few days weeping into each other's arms. Thanks to Anna's begging, Master John let me stay in the middle deck of the ship with my sister, but he made it clear I was only there to serve.

I was used to it, of course, but this seemed an extra punch to the stomach to have to serve my sister as though she were better than me.

Our cabin joined on to Master John's but his was mostly closed, him spending most days at sea behind his desk. Anna and I whiled away the hours sprawled on the floor, taking turns reading to each other, or sometimes drawing objects we found around the room. A vase with no flowers. A small bird made out of marble. Until Master John came in to check on us, then we would jump to our feet and I would pretend to be cleaning the table or pouring Anna some water. It was funny at first, but after a while I got tired of the pretence and I could tell Anna had too.

Our favourite thing to do though was drawing the captain who visited Master John's cabin once to invite him to dinner. He had heard our laughter and opened the door to our cabin to find me on the floor with Anna. He turned to Master John, glaring at him, and John promptly ordered me to do something useful with myself, thrusting an empty teacup at me. Remembering what Mama had said, I swallowed my pride and played the part, apologizing profusely, bowing my head, then stuck my tongue out as he left.

Master John caught me and reminded me sternly that it was because of my interference with Sarah that I was now in this position, and I was not to make things any more difficult for him.

That's when my dislike for Master John grew more than ever. He paraded himself as a good man, but when I really thought about it too long, I wondered how good a man he could be if he owned slaves. Even the ones he kept in his house and bought pretty dresses for.

When I told Anna my thoughts, as we lay in bed for the sixth day, she frowned at me.

"Ruth, I think that is a terrible thing to say when Papa protects you." She climbed off the bed in a huff saying she no longer wanted to talk to me about it, which set me off too and we both escaped to opposite sides of the room because there was nowhere else to go in a cabin. Our feud lasted until I got bored and drew her favourite picture of the entire journey: a picture of the captain looking like a mean ogre with bulging eyes and snarling teeth. This sent us into fits of giggles rolling on the floor until Master John opened the door and shouted at me.

Occasionally, when Master John was with the captain or having a rest, we sneaked out to explore the ship, ducking behind corners whenever we heard footsteps. It became like a game, pretending to be statues until whoever it was had passed.

We did our best to stay sane. Reading books, writing letters to Mama, me practising my writing while daydreaming of the grand life that awaited us in England. By day twenty, the sea had become so rough that we were too sick to do anything and were begging to see land again.

Over a month later, we arrived in England, at the port of Portsmouth, to a cold and grey welcome. The kind of coldness neither of us had ever experienced. Colder than the coldest winter nights in Jamaica. I had lost weight from all the vomiting from the rough seas and nothing could keep the cold out of my bones.

I wrapped my thin coat as tightly round me as I could, muttering through shivering lips, "Is this hell?"

England was not only cold, it was filled with more white people than I had ever seen in my life, and by the looks of it they had rarely seen anyone like me either.

Despite the cold, I tried to take in my surroundings as we made our way along the white-grey stone dock that tilted upwards above the water and on to flat ground.

A small man with a black moustache approached Master John, tilting his hat.

Master John pointed to his luggage. As the stranger reached for the cases, he spotted Anna, then me. He looked back at Master John, who told him we were with him.

"Even this one, sir?" he asked, but Master John was already climbing into a carriage. He inspected me before demanding, "Help me with these then."

He threw a sack at me and I caught it just in time. I glared at him, almost tempted to throw it back. The sack was heavy, probably filled with fruits.

"Step on it," the man shouted, "we haven't got all day." I bit my lip, dragging the bag over to the waiting carriage.

When the luggage was finally roped in tightly, I climbed into the carriage next to Anna and opposite Master John, who already had a newspaper open. The door closed and I shot Anna a furious glare.

"Are you comfortable there, Anna?" I hissed so Master John couldn't hear. Anna looked at my dirty clothes from carrying and lifting.

She turned to the window as the horse moved off.

"Yes I am, thank you. Isn't it lovely?"

I folded my arms against my chest, fuming. People barely looked at Anna whereas they stared at me. They accepted she was one of them, a luxury I did not have. I was beginning to think that England was not going to be the dream I expected. Maybe, like Jamaica, it would be Anna's.

I sank into the seat of the carriage, wondering what Mama was doing now, and if she missed us as much as I missed her.

What I noticed the most about England was how it changed so quickly from a busy overcrowded city with grey buildings and thick smells to empty spaces that stretched on for miles. The scenery kept both me and Anna mesmerized for most of the journey until I eventually fell asleep.

It was only the sudden stop of the horse that woke me. When I looked out of the window, we were outside a row of houses all attached to each other, spiralling upwards into levels like a ladder climbing to the sky.

"Oh!" I gasped craning my neck to see how far upwards the houses went.

We stepped out on to cobbled streets, and I was amazed at how grey it all looked. The houses were made of brown and grey stones. As grey as the sky and as grey as the road. The atmosphere itself was all grey and murky, like the after-effects of someone's cook burning the chicken and letting the smoke out into the yard.

"This is all one house?" I murmured, looking up.

Anna shook her head. "No, look, they all have front doors."

"Well maybe in England they have more than one front door," I retorted, still mad at her.

We followed Master John through a small gate and up three steps to the front door, where he took the door knocker in his hand and banged it against the black wood.

5.

ANNA

London, England
1781

A few minutes later, a pale-skinned woman with a long face and pointy nose opened the door. She was wearing a simple black dress with a high neck and long fitted sleeves. She had a white apron around her waist and a small white bonnet over her hair. She looked from Papa to me, to Ruth.

"Master Jonathan, welcome," she greeted him, trying to hide her surprise.

Papa pushed the door open and stepped past her, acknowledging her with a slight nod of his head.

"Ida, would you tell my sister I have arrived? Then take our cases upstairs."

The hallway was long and narrow and dark, matching the wooden walls and the floor.

There was no door at the end of the corridor to let the light in like there was in Jamaica and it felt even more gloomy than the outside. The dark walls were covered only by paintings. Many of them showed Papa sitting tall on a chair looking off to the distance. A few were of a woman and a child, the child sitting on the floor with her head on the woman's lap.

Ida took Papa's coat and hung it on a hook on the wall. She knocked on a door to the left and disappeared inside.

When Ida returned, she told Papa that Missus Edith was ready to see him.

Papa scoffed, shaking his head. "How accommodating of her."

The room was similar to Papa's office back in Jamaica. There was a deep burgundy love seat around a small glass table and two burgundy armchairs, one either side, facing the chairs was a large fireplace. Opposite the hearth were two windows side by side with twelve glass panels climbing upwards to the roof. Thick burgundy curtains were pulled back to allow the light in – though there wasn't much. It made me wonder if he had purposely styled his office to remind him of his home here in London.

Seated by the fire was a white woman who I assumed was Papa's sister, Missus Edith. She had yellow hair piled high on her head and wore a beautiful blue and white off-the-shoulder gown that would make the ladies back home jealous. Her skin was pale but her cheeks were red with the kind of powder I have seen before on the ladies who visit Papa.

A girl, a little younger than me, stood beside her, holding on to her mother's dress. She was the duplicate of her mother, from her pale skin to the extravagant dress to the hair. Except, on her, it just looked . . . silly.

Missus Edith opened her mouth as if to say something to Papa, then her eyes fell on Ruth and her mouth closed firmly. There was a moment of awkward silence as she looked Ruth over.

"Jonathan?" she said, her eyes not leaving Ruth.

Papa followed her stare. "Edith, this is Anna and Ruth; I sent you word about them."

She clutched at her pearls, her eyes travelling over me then Ruth again slowly. I moved closer to Papa.

"You said they were sisters."

Papa nodded, turning to look at us. "Yes, they are." He turned back to her and offered no further explanation. She waited for one but he gave none.

"And what do you want me to do with them? We have no need for more servants."

Papa sat in one of the armchairs, crossing his

legs, and I took this opportunity to rush to his side where I felt the safest.

Ruth threw me a glance that I could only interpret as betrayal for leaving her side. She could have stood beside Papa too, but I knew she wouldn't.

"You will look after them until I return," Papa said, pouring himself a small glass of port.

"Look after them?" Missus Edith gasped, her fingers moving from her pearls to her chest. "This is not an orphanage, Jonathan." She rose and stepped closer to him but her dress was so big it was as if she were floating. She leaned in towards Papa and hissed, "And what do you think my friends will say? What about the neighbours?"

Papa drained the last bit of port and stood. "The opinions of your friends has never been my concern. Now, I have been travelling for some time. I assume my room is ready."

He moved towards the door, and I hurried after him. We followed the servant, Ida, up the tall creaky stairs, feeling the eyes of Missus Edith and her daughter watching from below until we disappeared.

Ida told us to wait at the top of the stairs while she led Papa to a door at the end of a long corridor to the right. Ruth took my trembling hand in hers and squeezed it. I was grateful for it.

"Did you see the way they stared at us?" Ruth whispered, as we watched Papa enter his room and close the door. "Their eyes were bulging out of their heads like this." Ruth widened her eyes, turning her lips downwards, which made me giggle and almost forget how afraid I was in this new country with all these new faces. Ruth had a way of doing that, making me forget bad things. She could contort her face into the strangest shapes that would make anyone laugh.

I was used to dealing with slave owners and their families, but this felt different. Back home I had a role. I entertained and sometimes if Papa was feeling generous, I sat at the table with his guests. But here, I had no role, and without Papa, I was afraid of what would happen to me. I glanced at Ruth out of the corner of my eye; it was too frightening to think about.

Ida hurried towards us as though she was late for something. "Come," she said in a brash voice.

She bustled us further down the hall where there were two rooms opposite each other, next to a long narrow window at the end. She opened the door on the left. Inside was a bed, a desk by the window and a brown wardrobe.

I stepped into the room, looking around, and Ruth followed, but Ida stopped her. "Not you." I turned to

Ruth frantically and rushed back to stand beside her.

"We stay together," Ruth said urgently but Ida shook her head, already heading back towards the stairs.

"She stays. *You* come with me."

Ruth ran after Ida. "You can't separate us," she cried. When Ida didn't reply she dodged around her, blocking her path. "Ask Master John. He will tell you."

Ruth looked past Ida at me and her eyes were desperate for me to help her but my legs were stuck and I didn't think I could move them if I tried. What if I agreed with her and this woman banished both of us to the slave quarters – who would save us then?

Ida raised her hands to her waist, evidently angry. Ruth turned and hurled herself along the hall to the last door, banging on it repeatedly until Papa opened it, looking none too pleased at being disturbed.

"What is it, Ruth?"

"Master John, she is trying to separate us!" She was out of breath with panic. "You said we should stay together," she begged, "for Anna?"

Papa looked behind Ruth, past Ida, and his eyes fell on me. I felt a surge of guilt, as though I should have been the one begging him. What use was I if I could not stand up for my sister? I twisted my fingers nervously in front of me, but my eyes pleaded with Papa to help us.

"Sir, Missus Edith would not approve," Ida said earnestly. "She was adamant that the slave," she nodded to Ruth, "should be downstairs with the others."

Papa's eyes fell on Ida and narrowed. "Was she now?" he said. "Then that settles it – you will keep them together," he declared, then shut the door.

Ruth turned back to Ida triumphantly, who in turn shook her head and disappeared down the stairs.

I ran to Ruth as fast as my shaking legs could carry me and threw myself into her arms. Together, we rushed to the room before Ida returned to stop us.

Inside, I locked the door and sobbed in my sister's arms. I felt the same familiar emotions I had always felt: guilt for not standing up for my sister, but relief that we got to stay together.

"Anna," Ruth said, stepping back so I was forced to look at her. "Anna, you have to speak up," she said firmly. "When Master John is gone, they will only listen to you."

I nodded earnestly, biting the inside of my lip. I knew I should have spoken up more. Ruth relied on me, but I never had the right words like she did. I didn't have her bravery.

If only she knew how afraid I was of making things worse. Not just for me, but for her too.

6.

RUTH

At breakfast the next morning, Master John sat at the head of the table, his sister at the other end, and her daughter, Elisabeth, to the left of her. The table was long enough to hold fifty people and seemed almost as ridiculous as the table back home where Master John ate alone. I was about to sit opposite Anna when Missus Edith raised her hand.

"You will eat in the kitchen," she said.

My heart plunged and I looked to Anna.

Anna in turn looked to Master John. "Papa," she pleaded.

"She will eat with us," Master John said, barely looking up from his bowl of porridge.

Missus Edith set down her spoon and leaned forward.

"John, isn't it enough that I have taken them in? Now you want me to eat with her too?"

I caught Anna's bottom lip quivering. I glared at her until she took the hint, swallowing her tears. Anna had to learn not to fall apart in front of these people. She needed to be stronger. We were not in Jamaica any more. Here, she could not just fade into the background.

"She will eat with us," Master John repeated, nodding at me to sit. I pulled out a chair under the hard glare of Missus Edith, straightened my back against it, and signalled to Anna to do the same. Anna straightened her posture and together we both dipped our spoons into the porridge.

I swallowed the porridge and gagged, pulling a face. "A waah dis?"

Anna grimaced too but, unlike me, she maintained a dignified silence.

Master John stopped eating and looked at me. "Didn't your mother tell you to speak English?"

I turned to Missus Edith. "What is this, Missus Edith, please?" I said in perfect English. "Why is it so thick and heavy?"

I knew I was overstepping – and that, if she were here, Mama would not be pleased – but I couldn't help myself.

Anna tried to hide her smile, but Missus Edith

was not so impressed. Lips pursed into a thin line, she
ignored me and instead glared across the table at Master
John's lowered head, a smirk pulling at his lips.

A few days later, Ida helped Master John into his coat
as he got ready to leave for business in Liverpool,
warning us he may not see us again before he returned
to Jamaica. He placed his hat on his head and turned
to Anna, who had tears streaming down her face. She
threw her arms around him, bawling into his jacket.

"Please let me go with you," she pleaded.

Master John patted her head gently. "You know
you can't come, Anna, dear," he said softly. "It is safer
for you here."

I clutched a letter Anna had written to Mama from
both of us. It told her about the crossing, arriving in
England, the cold weather, the gloomy streets and the
squashed houses. I made Anna add a few white lies,
which I told her would stop Mama from worrying
herself sick.

*We are having a wonderful time. The house is filled
with laughter and music.*

*Papa has given us a lovely room, with our own
beds. Our window looks out to the street where there
are horses and carriages, and ladies with large hats.*

Papa's sister is pleasant and accommodating.
She has a daughter called Elisabeth who sometimes
does not understand what we are saying. Give kisses
to Sarah and William. We must go now; we have
much to do and see. We cannot wait to show it all to
you when you visit.
Your ever-loving,
Ami and Esi

Master John turned to me and held out his hand for the letter, but I hung on to it for dear life, as if handing over the letter meant giving up my life back home. He looked at me, frustrated, and reluctantly I let go.

We watched him climb into the carriage and close the door. As the horse trotted off, we waited to see if he would lean out the carriage and wave goodbye one last time. He didn't.

When we could no longer hear the hooves of the carriage in the distance, I grudgingly led Anna back inside and closed the door.

"Wipe your tears," I told her, "nuh let them see you cry."

Anna wiped her face and allowed me to take her hand. We turned, united, and faced Missus Edith who stood in the middle of the hall, her daughter behind her.

She told us to follow her into the sitting room, and

sat in Master John's chair, placing her hands in her lap. Elisabeth stood beside the chair, looking at us without expression.

"Now that my brother has gone, it is and always has been my duty to keep this house in order." Missus Edith looked at me and I held her stare.

"Now, let me be clear," she continued. "This is not the plantation house in Jamaica; there will be no running amok here. There will be rules and you will abide by them."

She paused, taking a breath for effect, only Anna's sniffles echoing through the silence.

"You," she pointed at Anna, "could very well pass for white, and so will be my daughter's companion. It is hard for her to make friends."

I stifled a laugh brimming in my throat. Glancing at Elisabeth, wearing a matching dress to her mother, bows in her hair and sucking her thumb as if she was three years old, it was easy to see why making friends was difficult.

"You will play with her, read with her, and when we have parties, which is often, you will help her make friends." Anna bowed her head in surrender. I elbowed her angrily. Why did Anna give up so easily?

"You." Her eyes moved to me and I braced myself. She sighed long and loud, shaking her head.

"Why my brother saw fit to bring you here, I will never understand, but here you are."

She sighed again wearily. "You will move into the servants' quarters downstairs and Ida will find work for you there. You will not enter these rooms or any of those upstairs ever again unless you are asked or have duties up there. You will eat and sleep in the servants' quarters, and you are only to be seen when you are required to serve guests."

I was already shaking my head. "No, we must stay together." I looked to Anna for help, pleading: "Tell her what your papa said."

Anna stared hard at the floor, biting her lip. "Yes," she whispered, "he did say that."

Missus Edith called Ida in and the maid opened the door. "Ida, take the negro's belongings into the servants' quarters." Ida nodded and left the room.

I rushed after Ida up the stairs, Ida picking up her pace but not getting much further ahead. I followed her into the bedroom I was supposed to share with my sister. "We stay together," I repeated, trying to block Ida's path as she threw my belongings into my small bag and headed for the door. Ida barged me out of the way and stormed down the hall. I followed, begging her, knowing full well without Anna beside me I would not be safe.

As we reached the bottom of the stairs Anna turned to

Missus Edith and whispered, "Please let us stay together."

"It has been decided," Missus Edith said, disappearing into the parlour.

I jostled with Ida. "Please," I begged frantically, "let us stay together." Ida held on tightly to my bag with one hand, hitting out at me with the other.

The commotion brought Missus Edith back into the hall. "You will let the housekeeper take your belongings downstairs or you will both find yourselves on the streets," she screamed at the top of her lungs. The jostling stopped and all that could be heard was Ida's heavy breathing.

Anna sank to the floor, distraught. She looked up at me through bleary eyes and I couldn't tell if it was worse being here or on the plantation being chased by the overseer. Finally I relented.

I got down on the floor next to Anna. "I'll be all right," I reassured her, wiping her tears away. I leaned in and whispered, "Be brave." Then taking a deep breath I got to my feet and followed Ida down the stairs.

7.

RUTH

The stairs to the servants' quarters were windy and
narrow and went all the way to the bottom floor.
The stairs led straight into a wide kitchen. Shelves
surrounded the room, filled with bottles containing
substances I didn't recognize. Between the shelves, the
stone walls of the kitchen were covered with pots and
pans hanging from nails. Underneath the shelves ran a
work table, and in the middle of the room a table with
benches. Scurrying around were a cook and the young
girl I remembered from breakfast. They stopped when
I entered, staring as though they had seen a ghost.

Ida marched to the other side of the kitchen and
continued down a dark and narrow corridor with a low
ceiling, me tripping along behind. She paused by a door

on the right and opened it, throwing my belongings inside. "You'll sleep here with the girl."

I stepped inside the room, if you could call it that. A tiny box with four walls and no windows. There was a bed against one wall, and a mattress on the other, with barely any room for anything else. I swallowed hard. Ida grinned triumphantly, as if she had won a battle I didn't know we were fighting. When she got nothing back from me but an empty stare, she turned on her heels and headed back towards the kitchen. Since there was nothing in the room to look at, I returned as well.

In the kitchen, the cook and the girl stopped what they were doing again and stared, except now there were also two men who had come in from the outside and a young boy.

"Well I never," one of the men said, chewing on a string of hay and taking me in.

"This is where you will eat, sleep and work," Ida said. "You don't go upstairs unless you've been told to and when you do go upstairs you don't talk to anyone, you don't give anyone eye contact, you don't do nothing unless they ask you, do you understand?"

I nodded slowly.

"You're nothing here, do you understand? You're nothing to nobody so don't give me no lip or I'll backhand ya." I met her eyes and she was deadly serious.

"You ain't nothing now, are ya?" she sneered before storming back up the stairs.

I listened to her heavy footsteps, using the moment to fight back tears. When Ida's feet became only a soft thud about our heads, I took a deep breath and turned to the audience in the kitchen. "What you all looking at?"

For a moment there was silence, and then the cook laughed, shaking her head. "You're a strange-looking one, but you'll do." She turned back to the stove. Slowly the men left to go back to work outside, but the boy stayed, fumbling to find a stool without dropping his gaze.

"Why's your skin like that?" he asked finally in a pitchy voice, his hair in his eyes.

I frowned. "Why is *your* skin like that?" I asked, pointing at him.

The boy looked down at himself and shrugged. "It's always been like that."

I nodded, pretending to think about his reply. "Hmm. Skin that has always been there; what a crazy thought."

The young girl laughed. "Come, I'll show you what to do," she said.

We headed to the far side of the kitchen, by the back door. The girl led me around a corner and into a large pantry with a high ceiling. It was filled with food, meat hanging from the ceiling and more bottles filled to the brim. She showed me where everything was kept, and explained what was served for each meal, including what the lady of the house liked for supper. "She won't ever ask for it, but if you don't bring it to her, she will get pretty mad," the girl said in an accent that was different from the others'.

"You talk different from everyone else," I said, interrupting her. The girl laughed again.

"I'm from Ireland; my mam works next door washing the lady's clothes. Sometimes she helps me here too if there's too much for me to handle. Which reminds me," she squeezed past me into the kitchen and went down the corridor towards the bedrooms. She stopped at a door on the left and opened it. It was filled with towels and sheets all folded on top of shelves that reached the ceiling.

The girl pulled something out carefully so as not to disrupt the pile. She handed me a pile of clothes, then went in for something else. "Your uniform," she said. "A dress, a pinafore, socks and shoes. Oh, and a cap to cover your hair." She glanced at my hair pulled into two cornrows.

"You can change in the room, but be quick – we have a lot of work to do."

I reappeared minutes later wearing a black dress to

my ankles with a white collar, a white apron and cap, dressed the same as the girl, who told me her name was Mary. Telling me to follow her, she carried a basket filled with sheets up the winding stairs.

When we reached the first floor, I took in a large gulp of air as if leaving a dungeon. It wasn't that downstairs was terrible place to be; I had seen worse. The slave quarters on the plantation, for instance. But upstairs in this house felt like the sky, and downstairs felt like a coffin it was so low.

We hurried to the second floor where the bedrooms were and Mary entered the room where John had slept. She placed the basket at the foot of the bed and began stripping the bed of its sheets. Down the hall I heard voices, then laughter. The louder of the voices I didn't recognize, but right after came the voice of Anna. I edged towards the door to listen.

"Can you start on the mistress's room?" Mary asked, bringing me back. "We will work faster that way and we might have some time to eat before the party."

I frowned. "Party?"

Mary struggled with the sheets in her hand. "The lady of the house is having a party tonight. She wants to show you off apparently."

"Me?" I said, pointing at myself, thinking I must have heard wrong.

Mary nodded before flicking the clean sheet out, and it hovered in the air before falling on to the bed. "You and your sister are the talk of the town."

I pondered this for a moment, wondering what could be so interesting about me and Anna that would warrant a party. I left her and went to the next room to be cleaned when I heard laughter again. This time curiosity got the better of me. I crept along the hall, past the stairs and to a room at the other end.

The laughter got louder and then I could hear my sister's voice clearly. I reached for the doorknob and turned it slowly.

"I wouldn't do that if I were you." Mary stood in the doorway of Master John's room. "If Ida finds you there, she will be furious."

I backed away from the door; the voice behind it had stopped. It had only been a few hours but already I missed Anna. We had never been apart this long. She was always around, always easy to find. Now here we were, in the same house but forced apart.

Reluctantly I walked back to the next bedroom to be cleaned.

Later, when we took the dirty sheets downstairs to the laundry, I asked Mary about Ida. "Why is she so angry all the time?"

Mary moved me away from prying eyes and

whispered, "You have to be careful who you talk to. Ida has ears everywhere and she always finds out if something has been said about her."

We handed the basket of sheets to the laundry maid and headed back upstairs to get the room ready for the party. Mary told me that Ida had been there for years, since she was our age, and she worked her way up. "She takes her job very seriously."

When we entered the drawing room, Mary stopped talking. The butler Cuthbert was waiting by the table, his gloved hands entwined in front of him. He barked orders as soon as we entered on how to set the table. This was something I already knew how to do. Back on the plantation, setting the table was one of my many jobs, so I didn't need Cuthbert or anyone else to tell me how to do it correctly.

While he was going through his long list of rules on how to set a table, I grabbed the white tablecloth that was folded on the table and spread it out, making sure there were no creases. I took the white china plates and placed each one in front of a chair, making sure it was centred. Then the cutlery: fork on one side, knife and spoon on the other. Then the glasses and napkins to the side, and candles and three baskets of flowers as centrepieces.

I finished triumphantly and turned to Cuthbert, who gave me a short nod that almost looked like approval.

He walked around the table examining the spaces between the plates and the glasses.

I whispered, "What he is doing?" under my breath and nudged Mary when he stopped and double-checked a plate.

He turned, still bent over the table, and eyed us both. Out of the corner of my eye, I saw Anna walk by, hand in hand with Elisabeth. A second before they disappeared on the other side of the doorway, our eyes met and there was a look of guilt as Anna's smile vanished.

Suddenly, I felt irritated with the amount of time Cuthbert was taking. Anyone would think the king was coming the way he was carrying on.

I sighed deliberately and Mary shot me a look but I didn't care. This was boring.

Cuthbert straightened his back and turned. With his gloved hands firmly by his side, he squinted at me, as if his eyesight was going, and maybe it was. Maybe that was why he had to get so close to the cutlery to check it.

"Is there a problem?" he asked. His gloved hands twitched by his side and Mary stiffened beside me.

But I was not afraid of him. I had faced much worse than a gloved man whose job it was to check the position of plates.

"Not at all," I said, in what Mama called my laughing voice. "I was just wondering if you had finished checking the table," She said I never smiled when I talked like that, but my eyes did.

The butler straightened his jacket, slow and deliberate, flattened his shirt with his hands and pulled off his gloves, one hand at a time. I was not afraid but I was on alert. It wouldn't be the first time someone calm had turned on me. Like the women who came to the plantation looking for Master John. They were all smiles, asking questions about him, until I said something they didn't like. I watched Cuthbert's movements, as I did when I didn't know someone well enough to know what they would do next.

In this strange country, I didn't have Mama to protect me and even though Anna was there, I couldn't rely on her helping either. Here, in this dark country, where we knew no one but each other, I had to protect us. Anna had to keep Elisabeth happy, and I had to keep them from sending me back home. I felt my stomach turn as I realized I had never had to survive on my own.

"Get out of my sight," he said and Mary didn't need telling twice. She grabbed my arm, dragging me out of the room and along the corridor.

Out of earshot she spun round to face me, horrified, "What were you thinking?"

I was about to tell her I didn't need to be told how to set a table, when I was distracted by a piano and someone singing.

The voice was sweet and light, like the sound of birds singing in the trees. I inched closer to the door, pressing my ear against it, and listened. It was the voice that had sometimes sung me to sleep. The voice that used to harmonize with mine as we skipped around the house when Master John was away.

Instinctively my fingers wrapped around the doorknob. Mary grabbed my arm. "No," she said in a frightened voice. "We can't go in there."

I turned to look at Mary, my eyes clouded with tears. "She's my sister," I whispered, unable to hold back any longer.

Mary searched my eyes then slowly let go. "I'll watch the stairs," she said, moving away.

Slowly I pushed the door open and the music filled the hall. Inside the dark room with its long heavy curtains and flowery carpet, Elisabeth sat at a black piano with Anna beside her. Anna rocked from side to side singing a song I had never heard and I wondered where she had learnt it because it didn't sound like anything we had ever sung before. I slipped into the corner of the room with my back against the wall, listening with some pain as Anna sang to the music Elisabeth was playing.

Then, forgetting I was not meant to be there, I moved closer, desperate to be a part of their world. I leaned against the piano, resting my chin on my hands.

The music stopped abruptly and Elisabeth glared at me. "You're not allowed in here," she said coldly.

I removed my elbow from the piano. "I was just listening,"

Elisabeth stood and the atmosphere changed. "I'm going to tell Mother you came in here." She moved around the piano, marching towards the door, but I cut her off.

"Don't do that," I begged, forcing a smile I hoped would change her mind. But Elisabeth was not so easy to convince and she attempted to pass me. I grabbed her by the shoulders to stop her.

"Get your hands off me," Elisabeth cried and suddenly I knew I had crossed the line. I had touched the mistress's child. That was unforgiveable. At home, to touch anyone white meant a whipping. Twenty lashes at least. I exchanged looks of horror with Anna, who was frozen, her hand over her mouth. I thought quickly.

Elisabeth was young and acted even younger. It was clear she knew nothing of the world. She looked as though she would be afraid of her own shadow.

I took a deep breath. "If you so much as say anything, I will find the biggest rat you have ever seen, and I will put it in your bed when you are asleep. But I will make sure the rat is hungry. I will find a hungry rat and you know what they say about hungry rats, don't you?"

I waited.

Elisabeth's eyes widened and her mouth parted as she shook her head slowly. I stepped closer until there was barely an inch between the two of us. "They say hungry rats are angry rats and angry rats will eat you whole."

Elisabeth looked at Anna, frightened. "Is that true?"

Anna glanced over at me and I gave her a nod. "Yes," she stammered, "it is true."

For a moment, we waited with bated breath. Finally, Elisabeth lowered her eyes.

"I won't tell a soul," she said quietly.

Anna threw me a triumphant look before waving me out of the door. She placed her arm around Elisabeth's shoulder, leading her back to the piano.

"It's all right, Elisabeth," she soothed, "I will take care of you."

And as I left, a pang of jealousy overwhelmed me.

8.

ANNA

I had always hated conflict. The thought of going into battle with someone was frightening because I was sure I would say and do the wrong thing, only to make it worse. I watched as Elisabeth sat down behind the piano as she had been before Ruth came in and changed everything. Her eyes scanned the keys, a small frown indented in her pale forehead, and I couldn't tell what she was thinking. If she was upset, or angry, or if she was already over the whole thing.

My heart was beating fast as if I had run an entire plantation and I placed my hand against my chest to slow it down. Words didn't form well when I was frightened. My head became cloudy and my thoughts disappeared into the mist. I couldn't form the simplest of sentences. I couldn't say what I really wanted to say. Sometimes I couldn't even remember my own name. It was as if fear had taken my mind hostage. I looked down at my hands and they were shaking.

"Are you coming?"

I looked up and Elisabeth was looking at me, eyebrows raised. No hint of any emotion that I recognized. I nodded quickly, hiding my hands behind my back and rushing to her side.

I sat on the bench beside her, shuffling up as close to her as I could get, and as her fingers danced along the keyboard I chanced a glance at her, this girl who was younger than me but with nothing to worry about but – I frowned; I had no idea what she worried about. Whether her hair was the way she liked it? Whether her favourite dress was laid out for her? I sank back and sighed. What a life to have, to never have to worry about your future. To never be afraid of being sold.

The music stopped abruptly. "Why aren't you singing?" she snapped, as if everything that had happened with my sister had been forgotten and all that mattered was this rotten song she wanted me to sing over and over until I was sick of every word.

I paused for a moment, then I looked at her, forcing a smile. I laid my hand on hers. "I have a better idea. Shall I read you a story instead? I'm very good at reading stories."

She broke into a smile and nodded enthusiastically. "Yes, I have a few favourites." She jumped to her feet and ran over to the bookshelves.

I looked down at my hands and they were still shaking but not as much. I took a deep breath and stood, forcing that smile I was so well known for, the one that put them all at ease. The one that told them I was on their side.

"Show me," I said as brightly as I could and followed her to the bookshelves.

I read to her for the rest of the afternoon until it was time for her nap. In the afternoon Elisabeth rested. It was her daily routine she told me, and I should remember it so she didn't have to tell me again. Upstairs, in her bedroom, I sat by the door watching as her maid unpinned her hair while she fidgeted like a toddler.

"I sleep for one hour," Elisabeth said, standing so the maid could undress her. "You mustn't let me sleep any longer because then the entire day will be gone." She raised her arms above her head. "Besides, it's Mother's party tonight and I don't want to miss it."

I cleared my throat. "Party?"

Elisabeth pulled on her long nightdress and beamed at me. "Yes, she's hosting a party for all the important people of London."

She climbed into her four-poster bed as the maid left, closing the door behind her. Elisabeth stared at me long enough for me to figure out what she wanted. I jumped to my feet and rushed beside her, pulling the sheets around her tightly.

"It's because of your sister," she said, snuggling into the pillow, already closing her eyes. "Mother says she is the talk of the town, that she is a trendsetter and soon everyone will have a slave for their parties too."

I stopped, my heart pounding against my chest.

"What do you mean?" I stammered but she didn't answer, her eyes firmly closed. I took a chance and shook her gently, knowing she could not have fallen asleep so quickly. "Miss Elisabeth," I whispered frantically, "what is it you mean?" but she still didn't answer, and she didn't open her eyes. I stood over her and placed my hands on my hips to steady myself. She was playing games with me. She knew telling me this lie would upset me. I was beginning to suspect Elisabeth was not as silly as she made out.

But what if it was true? What then?

I stumbled across the room and sat on the hard-back chair by the door where I was to stay until she awoke. I fidgeted with my fingers, staring at her, willing her to open her eyes so I could ask her what she meant. After ten minutes and no response, I sank back into the chair, my heart still racing. I didn't know whether she was lying or telling the truth. This was so hard without Papa. I felt my eyes welling up and I bit my lip hard to stop the tears from falling. I wanted so much to be brave but this was so difficult. More difficult than anything I had had to face so far. The weight of responsibility was solely on my shoulders and I was not strong enough. I was not Ruth.

I stared at the watch Elisabeth had given me to make sure she didn't oversleep. It was a gold pendant that opened as a watch with tiny hands and a small glass window. Sometimes the time blurred as tears streamed down my face, and other times my eyes grew tired and I almost fell asleep, but I was determined to not let her oversleep. I wanted to find out the truth the second she woke up.

Downstairs I heard bustling and lots of movement and I wondered if Ruth was below me, listening for me, wondering where I was. I yearned for her, for her wise words and bravery. She would know what to do. She always knew what to do.

The hands on the watch crept slowly round and finally reached four; I hurried to my feet and over to the bed. I shook Elisabeth's shoulders frantically as the door opened and the maid returned. She laughed. "You're going to have to shake her harder than that," she said, "she's a heavy sleeper."

I was not convinced she was even sleeping but shook her a little harder, although not so rough as to upset her.

"Miss Elisabeth," I whispered urgently. She didn't move. "Miss Elisabeth, wake up," I shouted and it came out so much more angrily than I had anticipated. The maid who was picking out Elisabeth's dress stopped and turned and I thought I had been too rough; now she would be angry.

Elisabeth stirred, rubbed her eyes and slowly opened them. She looked up at me and I waited to see if she was angry. "What is it?" she murmured, sitting forward.

"It's time for the party," I told her, pulling back the sheets. "Remember? You said there was a party tonight?"

She thought for a second and I felt I might have stopped breathing.

"Oh yes," she said, breaking into a smile, and suddenly she was full of life, jumping out of bed.

I watched as she spun around the room singing about how much she loved dressing up for parties. The maid waited for her to finish so she could dress her. I caught her as she spun. "So the party is real?" I asked urgently.

She pulled away from me and skipped over to the mirror where the maid was waiting. "Of course, it's real."

She looked at me through the mirror. "What will you wear? You should wear a dress that matches mine."

She beckoned me over and patted a stool next to her. I sat down and she took my face in her hands. "You should look just like me. We shall be twins." She opened the powder and started patting my face with it.

When she had finished, she smiled with satisfaction. "There," she said, "now we look like sisters."

I turned to look at myself in the mirror and my face was as white as a sheet, as though I had seen a ghost.

"Yes," I said numbly, "now we are the same."

9.

RUTH

The party began at eight, but I was summoned at seven. I had changed into a new dress and clean pinafore with black stockings and black shoes, but when I answered Missus Edith's call to her bedroom, she told me immediately that was not what I would be wearing.

Missus Edith's bedroom was particularly grand. There were ornaments on every surface, a large opulent dressing table and a wide dresser. There was a four-poster bed with posts that seemed to reach the ceiling, with at least two mattresses and gold sweeping curtains surrounding it.

That night, Missus Edith wore a long silk dressing gown and her lady-in-waiting, Elsa fixed her hair.

Through the mirror of the dressing table she observed me. "Your dress is over there," she said, pointing behind me.

For a moment I was confused until I spotted something hanging above the bed: a beautiful white gown. My heart picked up pace when I realized I was not going to be a servant tonight but a guest, the same as my sister. I rushed over to the dress and ran my fingers down it slowly in awe.

"Don't touch that," Missus Edith snapped. "You'll get your dirty fingers all over it."

I pulled my hand back. "But you said it was my dress."

Missus Edith nodded to Elsa who sighed and walked over to a chair by the door. She picked up a dress and threw it at me.

"This is your dress."

I unravelled the dress and held it up to the light. It was green with an obscene number of frills and a matching bonnet, the sort a small child would wear.

My heart sank a little that at my first English party I would not look as grand as everyone else, but more like an overgrown child. I would be laughed at for sure.

I wasn't sure which was worse: to wear this dress and be a laughing stock, or to serve my sister tonight as her servant.

I slipped out of my uniform and into the dress.

I observed myself in the mirror as Elsa pulled in the back and tied it. Missus Edith walked over and stood next to me. She regarded me through the mirror, her head to one side, moving around me slowly. "Put some bows on the side of her bonnet in her hair," she said. "It's too plain."

I had already done my hair that morning when I had learnt quite quickly people were fascinated by it. Downstairs, in the servants' quarters, Mary had watched me with such intensity I thought that maybe something was crawling out of it. Ida had also done the same when she barged into our room demanding why we weren't dressed. So, when Elsa stared at it confused, I took the bows from her and stuck them under the hat myself.

Ida barked rules at me as we made our way down the stairs.

Don't speak. No eye contact. No moving.

I couldn't make out why she didn't want me to move until we entered the parlour. A box covered in velvet cloth leaned against the right wall. Ida told me to stand on it. I looked at her, confused.

"Don't you understand English?" she snapped. "Stand on the box."

My heart fell to the pit of my stomach when I realized what I was being told to do. Back home, I would have pleaded, begged for anything else but this.

I would have had Mama to save me.

But here, all the way across the ocean, in a strange country, among strange people, I was alone. More alone than I had ever felt. Here I had no one. So I did as I was told and climbed on the box.

I stood like an empty shell, as Ida moved me this way and that, each time standing back to observe me before moving me another way. Eventually she settled on having me face the windows which were now covered by heavy curtains. She placed strings of beads around my neck, and an ornament of a monkey surrounded by fruit at my feet. The lamps in the room were lit by Mary, who kept looking over her shoulder at me until Ida shouted at her to get on with it.

Ida took my hands and clasped them in front of me, repeating the rules firmly.

No eye contact.

No speaking.

Do not answer any questions.

Do not move an inch, not even if a rat crawls up your leg.

"Do you hear?"

I did hear. Loud and clear. I was not a guest at this party. I was the entertainment.

Missus Edith entered the room with her first guests, Elisabeth and Anna trailing behind. Her guests were

Mr and Mrs Watson, a banker and his wife who lived a few roads away. Missus Edith brought them in, covering their eyes. She ushered them to the centre of the room, directly in front of me, excitedly telling them not to peek.

I did as I had been instructed, staring straight ahead, not making eye contact with anyone. Not Mary, not Ida and especially not Anna.

I found a particular spot to focus on to make the ordeal easier: a tiny peel of wallpaper that could be mistaken for a black dot, just above the window, at the edge of the curtain. The more I stared at it, the more I wondered how they could have allowed that tear to happen with all the servants they had in the house. But maybe it was because Missus Edith spent too much time on big glittery things, and not enough on the smaller things no one would notice.

Missus Edith dramatically told the Watsons to open their eyes, and she pointed at me excitedly. The Watsons oohed and aahed and moved closer to inspect me as though I were a painting.

"She is a present from my brother. A slave straight from the Caribbean," Missus Edith announced proudly, clapping her hands with delight. The Watsons moved even closer and I stared even harder at the peeling wall.

"Does she speak?" Mr Watson asked.

"Oh no." Missus Edith laughed. "She doesn't know how to speak; she's a slave." The Watsons laughed with her, but they continued to inch closer. Missus Edith told them to be careful as I was not house-trained.

I blinked away the feeling of nausea creeping up inside me.

"What do you use her for?" Mrs Watson asked, peering up at me. Missus Edith told them I didn't have much use except as an ornament to make her house look pretty. They laughed some more.

I felt a lump in my throat and the threat of a tear, but I held on to it for dear life. I begged myself not to break down.

Not here, not now.

I chanced a glance at Anna for some reassurance, and for a second our eyes met before Anna's eyes fell to her feet. Her face was as white as a sheet and so plastered with powder that it was all I could do to stop myself from demanding to know what she had done to herself. I returned my eyes to the peeling wall, trying desperately not to interpret my sister's look as one of betrayal.

The room filled with more people and more stares. Comments about my skin, my eyes, my nose, flew around the room.

How strong her legs look from work in the fields.

Does she speak?

Does she eat with her hands?

What do you feed her?

I would like to see her in slave clothes, with the chains. That would be more authentic, don't you think?

She must be indebted to you, Edith, for saving her.

I felt my soul leave my body and fly home. Not home where Walter drove the fear through everyone with a flick of his whip. Not home where friends worked for hours in the fields under the intense Jamaican heat for nothing but a wooden hut and scraps of food, and lashes on their back. Home, in Mama's arms, when she paused for a minute in her day, and she sat in a rocking chair in the kitchen with the door open, fanning herself from the heat.

Home was running to find her because I knew she only had minutes before she began work again. Home was sliding on to her lap like a baby, nestling into her chest and inhaling the smell of her while sucking my thumb. That was where my soul went that night. It flew above the grey clouds, across the ferocious seas and found itself back home in my mother's arms.

That was the beginning of a very long night. In hindsight, Mr and Mrs Watson were polite compared to some of the others.

Missus Edith had invited lots of very important and

rich people of London. The aristocrats she wanted to be like, the doctors, the theatre people, the ones slightly lower than her with fewer servants, less appeal, so she could show off and have them praise her. Within the hour the room was packed with chatter and excitement, and I was the main attraction. A harpist played in the far corner of the room, and a woman wearing the most oversized dress sang a shrill song that could only just be heard over the chatter, but no one paid her or the harpist any mind. They weren't here for music. They were here for me.

They prodded me with a wooden cane Missus Edith had provided for those who did not want to touch me with their own hands. They checked to see if I had five fingers on each hand and five toes on each foot but not once did my gaze move from that one spot on the wall. Not because that's what I had been told, but because I realized Ida's orders helped me to get through it, whether Ida meant them to or not.

By not looking at the people prodding and poking me, I could pretend it wasn't me they were prodding but someone else. Switching off was a talent I had honed from the plantation when someone would get whipped, or when Mama and I would go from having all the freedom in the house to being slaves again when Master John had visitors. I could do it when my sister was called into the dining room to sit at the table, but I wasn't. I could do it when the overseer tried once again to convince Master John to sell me. If I switched off from what was happening around me then I felt nothing, and nothing was the best feeling I could have right now.

When the butler called everyone into the next room for dinner, I stayed on the platform, hands locked in front of me, and two hours later when they returned, I was still there.

When the last person left the house, and the butler closed the door and locked it, Missus Edith finally spoke to me. "You can get down now," she said flatly.

It took some time for me to feel my feet. I stepped down slowly, cautiously, and felt the floor under me for the first time since I got up on that box hours ago. My legs were like jelly and almost buckled but I forced myself upright, refusing to go down now; not in front of Missus Edith.

She patted me on the back. "You did well," she said and I found myself almost feeling pride, that even though I was exhausted, hungry and could barely stand, at least I had pleased the wicked witch and I got to stay another day.

It was late before I was finally allowed to go to bed. After being forced to stand on a box, I was then ordered to tidy up the mess that had been left behind. By the time I fell on to the mattress on the floor across from Mary, I could barely keep my eyes open. I was drifting off to sleep when someone shook me. My eyes adjusted to the darkness to see Anna hovering over me, finger to her lips.

She beckoned me to follow her. I pulled on the first dress I found and tiptoed out of the door, through the kitchen, into the hall and up the stairs. The house was deathly quiet, and every step seemed to be on a creaking floorboard. The early morning light peered through the glass at the top of the door, guiding us.

Anna gently opened the door of the library and we slipped inside. She closed it softly and turned to me.

"What are you doing?" I whispered.

Anna's face was tear-stained and her eyes were bloodshot.

My heart sank. "What happened? What did they do?"

She threw her arms around me, burying her head into my shoulder. I wrapped my arms around her

"What happened?" I whispered again, terrified that something horrible had happened and I had not been there to protect her.

"Nothing," Anna's voice was muffled. "Not to me, to you."

I took a deep breath, realizing she was talking about the party.

"What has happened to you?" Anna asked. "Usually you would fight, but tonight you allowed them to do all those things to you."

My arms dropped to my sides. "I can't fight here." I said pointedly. "Not alone."

Anna avoided my eyes, moving around me and over to the walls filled with books. "Remember when we would read to each other at home?" she said, running her fingers along the spines. I sighed quietly, knowing what she was doing. What she always did. Avoiding trouble. It was frustrating when I needed her right then, but Anna was my sister. I felt responsible for her. Without Master John and Mama to protect her, the job was left to me. I had to protect Anna's place at the table, whatever the cost to me.

Anna gave me a wistful look. "Let's find one to read, and we can meet here every night and read to each other, just like at home."

I forced a smile despite feeling exhausted emotionally and physically.

"Yes," I agreed. "Let's do that."

I wasn't sure if I was agreeing to make her happy or if I really did want to come here and read every night. I felt drained and empty. My dream of coming to England and having a life that was equal to Anna's had been only that: a dream. I wanted to ask Anna if she was happy. If she enjoyed having Elisabeth treat her like a toy. If being at Elisabeth's beck and call was worse than what was waiting for us back home.

Anna scoured the shelves for a children's book but they were few and far between, which surprised Anna considering Missus Edith had a child. But I was not surprised at all.

"She doesn't like children," I said, matter of fact, which made us both chuckle. Anna eventually found one she liked and took my hand.

We squeezed into the high-backed chair in front of the shelves and opened the pages. Nestled against each other, I twirled Anna's hair, which was styled as a loose curl. "At least you don't look like a duppy any more," I said, smirking.

Anna stuck her tongue out. "They made me do it," she said. I forced a smile to reassure her I was not mad, but I couldn't help but wonder if they really did make her or if she wanted to.

10.

ANNA

It was Mary the maid, the one who worked with Ruth, who found us some hours later wrapped in each other's arms. She said she had woken to Ruth's empty bed and went looking for her, frantic that she was getting herself in trouble again, and she was right to think that, she said, because there we were, getting in trouble again. She apologized to me for overstepping.

"I don't mean to be rude," she said. "But if the missus finds you here, she will be very angry." It was the first time anyone had spoken to me as if I was somebody and I instantly took a liking to her.

We said our goodbyes and separated on the landing. Ruth followed Mary down the stairs while I climbed the stairs begrudgingly to find Elisabeth, and I couldn't help but be jealous that Ruth seemed to have made a true friend and not one she was forced to babysit.

When I reached the top of the stairs, I could already hear Elisabeth. Her voice travelled from her mother's room, shrill and sharp. It always surprised me how such a small girl had such a loud voice.

I moved towards Missus Edith's bedroom and rested my ear against the door to listen. Elisabeth was begging her mother for a pony.

"And what would you do with a pony?" Missus Edith said wearily. "You would be bored of it in minutes and then what?"

Elisabeth continued whining, "I wouldn't, Mother, I swear, and Anna will help me. She can make sure I'm safe and she will keep it clean."

I stepped away from the door and headed to the end of the hall, still hearing Elisabeth's voice in my head. I rushed into my bedroom and closed the door behind me, sinking on to the floor. I laid my head in my hands, worn out at the thought of spending another day entertaining this spoilt girl who now wanted me to look after her horse!

I thought of home. The vast greenery. Mother singing; Ruth begging me to play hide and seek when Papa was locked in his office. I felt the tears stream down my face and I allowed myself to cry. I cried into my hands, my body shaking as I thought about how much I missed home. How much I missed Mother.

I heard the bedroom door open and climbed to my feet. I gently opened the door a crack and peered down the hall. Elisabeth and Missus Edith were heading for the stairs.

"Where is Anna?" Elisabeth said, looking around. She stopped and turned. "Maybe she's in her room."

"She'd better not be," Missus Edith said haughtily. "She seems to think she is here visiting, not here working." Elisabeth turned back and followed her mother down the stairs.

I waited until I could no longer hear their footsteps then I stepped out of the room and tiptoed down the stairs after them. I passed the sitting room where I could hear Missus Edith talking and Elisabeth whining. I tiptoed by their door and into the library, where I knew Missus Edith never ventured and Elisabeth only went when I was with her. I closed the door quietly and heaved a deep sigh of relief.

This was the only room where I felt safe. It wasn't my bedroom, where Elisabeth constantly barged in without knocking, as though I had no right to privacy because I was living in her house. I didn't feel safe in that room. I barely slept, and when I did it was out of exhaustion because my eyes could no longer stay open watching the door.

When I did fall asleep eventually, I had a recurring dream that Elisabeth and her mother planned to send me away, and only needed me to fall asleep to put their plan into action.

Every night I dreamt of them sneaking into my room and taking me when I was defenceless and deep into sleep. So, every night before I got into bed, I put a chair behind the door. It wasn't strong enough to keep out someone determined to get in, but it would be enough to wake me. I learnt that from Mama. She always slept with a chair behind the door. Papa didn't know this but after he came into my room to say goodnight, I would sneak downstairs to the back of the house and into Mama and Ruth's bedroom. I would slip into my sister's bed and Mama would close the door behind me, placing the chair under the handle. In the early morning she would wake me and send me back upstairs before Papa noticed I had gone.

I picked up the book Ruth and I were reading last night and snuggled into the chair, tucking my legs under me and resting my head against the back of it.

I had read one chapter when the door opened quietly. I looked up, startled, half expecting to see Elisabeth looking for me but instead it was Ruth. I sat up suddenly. "What's happened?"

Ruth closed the door softly and turned to me, frantic. "I can't do this," she said earnestly. "Can't you say something? You don't seem to be doing anything to help us."

I slumped back into the chair. Her disappointment in me hurt.

"I don't know what you mean," I said quietly, avoiding her glare. I heard her sigh in annoyance.

"Talk to Missus Edith. Tell her we have to be together. Tell her Master John said so."

"We tried that already."

"No, Anna, *I* tried that already," she hissed. "You haven't done anything but prance around in pretty dresses playing games and powdering your face. Meanwhile I am slaving away downstairs."

I knew she would bring up the powdered face. I had been preparing for it from last night. At the party, she gave me a look of almost disgust, as though I had betrayed her. I had prepared myself for the onslaught after. For her to call me a traitor, for her to jump to conclusions without knowing the truth. But she had said nothing until now and somehow it hurt more than if she had said it last night.

I folded my arms against my chest. "I'm trying, Ruth, but it's not easy."

"Try harder!" Ruth shouted so loudly her voice bounced off the walls. I jumped to my feet and rushed across the room, clasping my hand over her mouth. I watched the door nervously, every sense alert, waiting to hear a door open downstairs and then footsteps. My heart pounded against my chest as I thought about what could happen if we were found here, together. After a few minutes when no one came, I let go of her and stepped back. I couldn't keep doing this, doing things we weren't supposed to, hoping we wouldn't get caught. It set my nerves on edge.

"We can't keep doing this," I said, frustrated. "If they find you, they will send you back."

When she didn't answer I stopped pacing and looked at her desperately. Her eyes were filled with hurt. "Send *me* back?"

My heart dropped as I realized my mistake. "Us," I corrected myself quickly. "They will send us back."

"And is that such a bad thing?"

It was the first time I had heard Ruth say she wanted to go back and it startled me, knowing what we would have been going back to. I took her hand and tried not to let her see how afraid I was that she seemed to be giving up. "Mama said Walter would sell us. He was determined, remember?"

She closed her eyes, her shoulders slumping forward; I had never seen my sister like this. She was always a fighter, but it all seemed to have gone. "What can be worse than this? What can be worse than being poked and prodded like an animal?"

There was nothing I could say to that. The things they had made her do last night made me sick to my stomach. It was all I could do to have stayed in that room and not run. But if my sister no longer wanted to fight, what would happen to us now?

She sighed, as if knowing what I was thinking. "We are going to speak to Missus Edith again."

I heard myself take a sharp breath. "What will we say?"

She looked at me sternly. "You, Anna, you will say what your father promised. That we should be together and treated equally."

I thought of all the reasons why this would be a terrible idea. How we were already on thin ice with Edith. How she was looking for any excuse to send us home. I thought of all the ladies who came to the plantation and how awful they got when I asked a question they didn't like or suggested that Papa might be too busy to see them.

Unlike Ruth, I knew women like Edith. I had eaten with them, sat in the parlour listening to their gossip until they were tired of seeing me and wanted me gone. They were erratic. Laughing one minute and like the devil the next. I was never quite sure if it was the tight corset or the heat that made them that way. But they were unpredictable and, like Papa said, there is nothing more dangerous than a person you can't trust.

My hands were shaking when Ruth led me out of the library and along the quiet hall. They were still shaking when we stopped outside the parlour door and she gave me a reassuring nod. I took a deep breath, but it did nothing to calm my nerves. I turned the handle slowly, praying for some reason it was locked, but it wasn't, and turned easily.

Missus Edith was sitting in Papa's chair, sewing, while Elisabeth sat across the room from her, mimicking her mother with her own sewing kit. They both looked up when we entered; their blue eyes followed us as we walked into the middle of the room. As if sensing something she was not going to like, Missus Edith placed the sewing in her lap and her eyebrows knitted together. Ruth nudged me forward and with shaking legs I took centre stage.

I cleared my throat and clasped my hands into the folds of my skirt. I thought about all the times I had had to speak in front of people who scared me, which was a lot because Papa was always having visitors. I thought about how they would look at me with suspicion as they tried to figure out my place and my relation to Papa. I thought about how when I smiled their frowns loosened and their eyes rounded as though I had cast a spell on them by just smiling. So that's what I did; I put on my best smile and I spoke as well as I could, without the Jamaican twang that so often crept in, that twang which so often disappointed them. I spoke like my father.

"My sister and I have been so grateful for your hospitality," I started, smiling sweetly, but only Ruth knew the smile was forced. That the tension in my face was to stop myself from shaking. I cleared my throat when the silence became deafening. "You have been nothing but accommodating to us." I felt Ruth glaring at me but I tried to tune her out; it was the only way I was going to get through it.

"It's just that my sister and I have never been apart. We have always been together in everything; Papa made sure of that. He wanted us to stay together; that's why he brought us here, together." I was rambling, I knew, but I was desperate to get through to them and so far, they were showing no signs of being moved. I took a chance and sat next to Edith. "My father said the first night we arrived that we should be together."

"What exactly do you expect from me?" Missus Edith snapped, an eyebrow raised.

I took another breath to calm my nerves. "For my sister to be with me. We would be no trouble. We can share a room, and we would both look after Elisabeth and attend to anything you need."

There was a short laugh from Missus Edith, and she picked up her sewing as though that was the end of it. I glanced at Ruth, confused and a little desperate. She gave me a reassuring nod.

"Is that a yes?" I asked Missus Edith cautiously.

"The negro will remain in the basement with the other servants because that is where she belongs, and she should count herself lucky that she even gets that," Missus Edith said, sewing placidly. "I know of many places that are far worse, including sending you both back home where I have heard a good friend of yours eagerly awaits your return." She shot me a calculated look and I instantly knew she was referring to the overseer.

"Yes, I know everything, so if you think you can spin me a story of love and happiness, you clearly do not know me well." She shifted away from me in her seat. "And if you do not like it, mulatto, you can join your sister in those servants' quarters. Or better yet, I can send you both back to the hell from which you came."

My heart fell to the pit of my stomach and I felt

myself crumble. She did not buy it. She did not accept me as one of them. She had called me a mulatto, a word that I had only heard once before.

One day, when Ruth and I were running through the field, playing catch, a young field slave had yelled it at me. That night, I had asked Mama what it meant. Even now, I could picture the look of horror on her face. She had said that it was a mean, hurtful word used to describe people who have parents with different skin colours. People like me.

Missus Edith had returned to her sewing. I was dismissed.

I swallowed the tears, standing slowly, carefully so as not to give away that I was falling apart. I walked to Ruth and she stopped me, lay both her hands on my shoulders and pushed my shoulders back. Then she lifted my chin, took my hand and led me to the door.

"Elisabeth has brought the previous incident to my attention. If I find out you have been in my library again, I will do more than send you home," she threatened.

Elisabeth stood by her mother, smirking. Despite Ruth's threats, Elisabeth had told on us.

Outside in the hall, Ruth tried to calm me down, but I was distraught. "She told on us!" I paced the hall, frantic at what this could mean. "Why did she do that? She promised me. She promised me she wouldn't tell, and I believed her."

Ruth pulled me away from the door, out of earshot. "Well, that was your first mistake," she said, and I felt like she was telling me off. Her expression changed and she looked at me with pity, as though I were a small naïve child.

"We have to leave," she hissed.

I looked at her, horrified. "Leave? And go where?"

"Mi no know," she replied, frustrated, "but anyt'ing is better than being forced to stand on a box and be prodded by strangers."

I sighed, looking away. I knew she was right, but what could I do?

Ruth looked infuriated by my lack of response. "Yuh can't understand dat because it no 'appen to yuh but it is mi life, Anna," she said, slipping back into Patois.

I turned away, folding my arms tightly across my chest.

"Maybe yuh nuh want things to change. Just like back home when yuh had nothing to lose, because yuh think yuh one of dem," Ruth spat. "But yuh not, no matter 'ow pale yuh skin or how good yuh read an' write. Yuh neva gon' be."

I unfolded my hands and clenched them by my sides.

"Maybe they are nice to me because I am nice to them,"
I snapped. "Maybe you should try it."

I picked up my dress and hurtled up the stairs and as
far away from her as possible. I ran into my room and
shut the door, wiping the tears away with the back of
my hand.

For the second night running, Missus Edith held a
party. Word had spread further afield of her surprise,
her new ornament. Missus Edith had become what she
always wanted, what she had strived for her entire life.
She had become the talk of the town, and her parties
were the place to be.

Once again, I sat inside Elisabeth's room, on the
chair beside the door as she slept. I watched the hands of
the clock slowly turn. Slower than the last time. When
Elisabeth had called me to her room, she mentioned
nothing of the incident in the parlour. Instead, she
talked excitedly of another party her mother was
holding, "Because the last one was so popular, she had
to do another."

I had smiled weakly; now all I could think about
as she slept was Ruth and what they were putting her
through. I would have to stand there in the room while
they prodded her and leered at her and there was not a
thing I could do.

I felt sick.

If only Ruth and I had parted on friendlier terms –
I knew I wouldn't get an opportunity to apologize now
until the night was over.

When the party began, Missus Edith called
Elisabeth and I out into the hall to make our entrance.
Through the banister I could see the hall downstairs
was full, as people tried to get into the parlour.

I pressed my hand against my stomach to stop the
gurgling feeling of sickness that seemed to be getting
worse and worse.

Missus Edith and Elisabeth held on to each other
excitedly, waiting for the last person to cram into the
room before they made their way down the stairs
slowly, smiling and waving.

Missus Edith stopped to compliment everyone. "Oh
look at you, where did you get that from? It's divine."
She moved slowly along the hall and I was forced to
trail behind them, not knowing where to look or what
to do with myself whenever they stopped.

We entered the parlour to applause, and out of the
corner of my eye I saw my sister on the podium but I
didn't look because I feared it would be the last straw
to the nausea seeping up my throat.

I separated myself from Elisabeth and Edith,
pushing my way to the back of the room, out of

sight and hopefully out of mind.

I stood against the wall by the window, forced there because there were so many people, hands clasped in front of me, staring hard at my fingers, not daring to look up.

"Do you not care to look?" a voice said near me. I glanced to my left and it was a boy dressed in a tailored suit as though he were an adult. He pointed to the front of the room as if I didn't know what he was talking about. "Do you not care to look?" he repeated. His smile was wide and his eyes excited, as though someone had just offered him his favourite meal. I shook my head, returning my gaze to my hands.

"Why? Are you not entertained?" I tried to close my ears and block him out. I didn't want to bring any attention to myself or say anything that might upset Edith's guest. I sank further into the curtains hoping he would get bored.

"My name is Arthur; what's yours?" He offered me his hand and if I had learnt anything from Papa, it was that it would be rude to ignore an outstretched hand. So I took his hand loosely, but as I did so I felt someone's eyes on me, and despite my rule I looked and locked eyes with my sister. She was dressed head to toe in rags, like the children we saw on the London streets our first night. They had sewn fruits into the cloth, and it was dragging her down because her shoulder leaned to one side. Her eyes were brimming with tears as she looked at me accusingly, as if I had committed the ultimate betrayal. I pulled my hand away and pushed through the crowd and out of the door. I ran up the stairs and just about managed to reach the bathroom before I was sick in the basin.

11.

RUTH

"What do you mean, you want to go somewhere?" Mary asked as we folded sheets in the laundry room. She threw one end to me, her face suspicious. I didn't want to tell Mary everything just in case she couldn't be trusted. I couldn't risk Missus Edith finding out my plans.

"Well, there must be more places to work than here," I said carefully.

Mary didn't buy it. "You want to work somewhere else?"

I shook my head. "No."

We fell silent, folding, and I avoided her inquisitive eyes.

"Because I would want to leave too if I were you," she said.

I packed the sheet into the basket and turned away from her to grab another.

"I don't want to leave," I told her flatly. "I like it here."

The house was quiet for most of the morning. Servants went about their duties almost silently so as not to disturb Missus Edith, who had a headache. I didn't see Anna at all despite working upstairs for most of the morning. At about noon, the atmosphere had changed and everyone started rushing around. Ida banished me to the scullery again.

I only realized I was being hidden away when Mary was called upstairs twice but not me. My first instinct was to blame it on Elisabeth, but after my sister's performance last night, I began to think it might be Anna who had asked for me to be sent down here.

Servants ran around gathering tablecloths and glasses, then rushed back upstairs. Normally I was given the brunt of the labour, but for some reason, whatever was happening upstairs, no one wanted me involved.

I tried to catch Mary on her third trip down into the kitchen. "What's going on up there?"

Mary grabbed a silver tray with a pot of tea and two teacups. "It's the master; he's home," she said as she carefully carried the tray up the winding stairs.

I was frozen in the middle of the kitchen, my wet

hands dripping on the floor. Master John had arrived. I didn't even know he was coming. This was the best news I could have had. I didn't have to run away. I could speak to him.

Maybe he could take me home and find a way for me to live on the plantation safely. Or maybe Mama and I could run away to the mountains where plenty of slaves had escaped. They had built their own village and lived free.

The cook scolded me at the pool of water developing at my feet.

"You better clean that up before Ida sees it or she will make your life not worth living." She tutted. I rushed to the scullery to find a mop, and tried to think of a plan to get to Master John. Minutes later I re-entered the kitchen with the mop. I cleaned the floor, absentmindedly watching the stairs.

When Mary returned for more biscuits, I seized my chance. I offered to take the tray from her.

"Please," I begged. "Let me take it up there."

Mary shook her head, frantically trying to pull the tray out of my grasp. "You will cost me my job," she said. "Ida has made it clear. You are not allowed up there."

But I was not about to let go, even if it meant scuffling on the floor. "Please, Mary." I gave her a look of desperation. Mary's grasp loosened slightly, but it was enough for me to swipe it out of her hand and rush up the stairs.

Mary called after me, "You will get us both in trouble." But nothing was going to stop me. It was my only chance to speak to the one person who could save me from this hell. I had no idea how long Master John would be here, or if I would get another chance.

Master John was sitting in his usual chair; the one Missus Edith took over when he was gone. To his right sat Anna, who seemed surprised to see me, which made me twice as mad that she hadn't let me know her father was back. Two men sat across from Master John. One, tall and white, was wearing a grey wig and ill-fitting clothes. But it was the second man who stopped me in my tracks.

He was a small man, dignified, with a full face and small smiling eyes. He wore a small tailcoat, a fitted deep-green waistcoat and a white neckcloth. But more than that: he was black. As black as me, not passing like Anna. He looked as though he had just come off the boat too, except he wasn't dressed like anyone from back home. He wasn't dressed like a slave. He was in knee breeches, black boots and had a top hat on the table beside him. He was dressed the same as the other two men, as if he was one of them, but he looked like me. I almost dropped the tray.

"Close your mouth, Ruth," Master John said sternly. I clamped my mouth shut but still couldn't take my eyes off the gentleman who looked like me. He tipped his head in my direction and gave me a broad smile as Master John and the other man returned to their conversation.

I opened my mouth to say something, but nothing came out. I tried again, my mouth opening and closing like a fish. Behind me the door burst open and Ida rushed in.

She shot daggers at me, grabbing me by the arm. "Outside, now."

Seeing my opportunity slipping away, I turned to Master John.

"I want to go back home with you," I blurted out.

The chatter stopped and all three men looked at me as I tried stubbornly to stop myself from being yanked out.

Ida apologized profusely. "I am very sorry, gentlemen. She is wicked, full of mischief!" she said, squeezing my arm so tight I winced. "I will deal with her."

I looked pleadingly at Master John, desperately digging my feet into the carpet.

"Let her stay," the dark-skinned gentleman said. "I have lots to share with her about her new country."

Master John looked to the other man – the white man – who nodded.

He reflected the nod back to Ida. "Leave her."

Reluctantly, Ida released her grip, but not before giving me an extra-tight squeeze. She flashed the gentlemen a forced smile before leaving.

I turned back to the room and found my sister beaming at me. I ignored her and rushed over to the gentleman who had come to my aid.

He told me his name was Francis Barber and that he was the manservant of Master Samuel Johnson, the white man who was deep in conversation with Master John.

"You don't look like a servant," I observed as Anna joined me, sitting at his feet.

He laughed gently and nodded. "Yes, you would be right. Servant is my title, but I am more than that. Samuel and I are friends."

Despite having fallen out with each other the day before, I exchanged a look of disbelief with Anna. We fired questions at him: *why were they friends, where did he live, how did he get to England, did he like it here.*

"Do you want to leave?"

He was holding his hands up to our questions but lowered his hand when I asked the last one.

He looked at me steadily. "Do you?"

I nodded with the most certainty I had ever had. "Yes, I want to go home."

"But the overseer will try to sell us if we go home," Anna interrupted.

"*Me*," I corrected her. "He will sell me."

"Mama said he would sell both of us," she said quietly.

"She only said that to make me feel better," I snapped. "No harm will ever come to you on that plantation, or anywhere else for that matter. You know it, I know it and Mama knew it too."

A silence fell over us and only the gentle hands on our shoulders from Francis broke it.

"You have to search for pieces of joy wherever you are," he said to me. "This is where you are, for now."

My bottom lip trembled. "There is no joy here for me," I told him.

For a moment, Francis was silent. He squeezed my arm, then leaned forward and whispered, "There are others, you know. We meet most evenings at the local tavern; men, women, children, just like you and me."

"And your master allows you?" Anna asked, wide-eyed.

Francis laughed, nodding his head. "Yes. This place is filled with conversations about our day, politics, what is going on in the rest of the world, how we can help each other."

I listened in disbelief that there were others like me. I felt a small tug of hope.

"There is often music, poetry, dancing," Francis continued, but I was no longer listening. All I was thinking about was what he had said before; the most important words I could have heard that day. They helped each other. That was it. That was how I was going to escape. I didn't know how, or when, but if these people at the tavern were anything like the man sitting in front of us, they would have the answers.

An hour later, we stood in the hall, watching Francis leaving with his white master through the front door. Master John waved them off from the doorway.

"We have to go there," I whispered under my breath. Anna shook her head, moving her hand from side to side in a wave, the way she had seen the rich ladies do.

"Missus Edith would never let us go; you know that."

"Yes, Anna," I said smartly. "I do know. That is why Missus Edith would not know we were going."

"And how do you plan to go, if Missus Edith will not allow us?"

I cocked my head to the side, frowning. "I don't know, Anna; how will we leave if Missus Edith will not allow us?" I tapped my chin, pretending to think.

John closed the door and walked by us, re-entering the parlour. "You're making fun of me," Anna said haughtily. "You know I don't like it when you do that."

"Well maybe don't ask silly questions that you can answer if you just think about what you are saying for one minute," I snapped. Everything Anna did was annoying me. It was like she didn't take any of this seriously. Anna turned to follow her father, but I grabbed her arm. "So are you coming? We can go tonight. Missus Edith always goes to bed early. We can sneak out and be back before she even knows."

"But Papa is only here for a few days before he really does leave to go home," Anna said, glancing into the room where her father had returned to his newspaper. "I want to spend as much time with him as possible, don't you?"

"I don't think your father would care if I spent time with him or not," I said, trying not to think of what was going to happen to me after Master John left. Even more reason to plan our escape. "But you're not going to watch him sleep, are you?"

Anna gave me a dry smile. "You're making fun of me again. If you want to get into more trouble than you are already in then I can't stop you. I can only tell you that I don't think it is worth the trouble."

I stiffened, furious. "My freedom is not worth the trouble?"

Anna shook her head quickly. "That's not what I meant; what I meant was—"

"What you meant was, your life is good and you're not willing to change it," I interrupted her "Not even for me."

I turned on my heels and stormed down the hall.

12.

RUTH

I didn't go downstairs where the other servants were; instead I used the opportunity of having Master John home to sneak into the library where I could be alone. I closed the door quietly behind me and leaned against it, trying to slow my breath. When I opened my eyes to the room, I realized this was the first time I had really been all alone since I arrived in this country.

My sister's laughter pierced through the walls and the separation between us felt like a thousand miles rather than one room.

I sank into the velvet chair with a book randomly chosen from one of the shelves. I loved Anna dearly, but her biggest problem was her denial of what was happening around her. It was that very truth that continued to separate us, because even if Anna knew in her heart that the way I was treated was wrong, she would never admit it out loud. Because to admit it was to betray the very people who kept her alive.

I tucked my legs under me and tried to focus on the words in front of me. But the more I heard Master John's playful voice and Anna's laughter, the more alone I felt. I stared hard at the pages, skimming them as if I were reading every word, when in fact I could not have told you a single thing about the story. Really, I was just taking the chance to hide from Ida and Edith.

I was here so the cook wouldn't clip me around the ear for putting the pans in the wrong place. Or so I wasn't watching the coachman as he trudged on to the newly cleaned floor with his dirty shoes, only to be told I was to clean it again. If I stayed here, in the library, I would not have to deal with Mary's questions about my skin and if it was the sun, or was I born that way. What it was like to be a slave in the West Indies, or to have the stable boys gathered at the window, watching me like I was a show and they were the audience. But most of all, I would not watch Anna pretend that to be here, in this house, was a much better choice than to be anywhere else with me.

When the laughter subsided next door, I assumed Master John had asked for his reading time because I heard the soft voice of Anna telling him goodbye. John often liked to spend his afternoon reading the latest newspapers. It was his time to rest. He had a small glass of whisky, and locked himself away for at least an hour when no one was allowed in.

"Not even if the house is on fire," he would say.

This would make me and Anna laugh because we always imagined Master John sitting in his chair with his legs crossed at the knees, reading his paper while the house burned down around him.

I listened to the door closing, and Anna's soft footsteps along the hall. I thought about calling her and inviting her in, but something had changed between us that I no longer wanted to fix. So, I stared hard at the pages in front of me.

Her footsteps went quiet and so did the house. It was the most silence I had experienced since I arrived. I listened out for Ida or Missus Edith, the clatter of dishes or the running of footsteps as Mary was called yet again to Missus Edith's room to take off her shoes, or fan her while her personal maid undressed her.

The silence was unsettling, and I was considering leaving when the door opened. I was quick on my feet but it was too late; Elisabeth walked in with Anna close behind her. Both stopped suddenly, Anna almost falling into Elisabeth. Anna looked at me with dread as

Elisabeth's laughter turned sour.

"You are not supposed to be here."

I quickly put the book back into the bookcase. "I know, I'm sorry." I attempted to redeem myself, but it was obvious from the start Elisabeth would not be sweet-talked.

"Mother said you were never to come in here again."

"Maybe she was asked to," Anna tried. She looked over at me desperately. "Were you asked to, Ruth?"

I thought quickly on how to answer. The obvious answer would have been to lie, if only to calm Elisabeth down in the moment. But what if Elisabeth had checked out the lie, what then? Would the punishment have been worse? Most likely.

"Ruth?" Anna prompted me urgently, but it was too late.

Elisabeth turned on her heels. "I'm telling Mother."

Both Anna and I shouted "No!" and Anna spread her arms out, blocking the door.

"Elisabeth," she pleaded, "I thought we were friends?"

Elisabeth glared at her. "Mother says we are not friends," she retorted. "She says you are my companion, and you are to do as I tell you."

A look of hurt shadowed Anna's face and I think it may have been the first time she had been told she was not one of them. I rushed to her defence, pushing myself between the two of them. I glared at Elisabeth in the same way I had the other day when she had threatened to tell. For a moment Elisabeth's demeanour dropped and she looked afraid.

I stepped closer, staring her dead in the eye to really bring the point home, although what the point was, I didn't know, just as long as Elisabeth was afraid.

But then Elisabeth raised her eyes to meet mine and she folded her arms across her chest. "Move out of my way."

I was so startled it hadn't worked that I didn't have time to think of what to do next.

"Move out of my way or I will scream," she warned. "I will scream so loud that the whole street will hear, and when they find you here, in this room with me, they will hang you." This time it was she who leaned in, her lips snarling, teeth bared. "Have you ever seen someone hanged? I have. They will hang you in the town where everyone can watch, even your sister." She glared at me. "Now move, servant."

My face paled and I moved to one side, allowing her to open the door. As soon as she stepped into the hall, she started to run, screaming for her mother. Anna looked at me, mortified, before running after her, promising everything and anything to quieten her. Elisabeth ran up the stairs and we followed not far behind, knowing full well where she was heading.

At the top of the stairs Ida appeared out of nowhere and blocked my path, demanding where was it I thought I was going.

Anna tried to explain but Ida refused to move. In the end it was Anna who uttered the words that finally moved her. "My father is downstairs and if you do not move out of the way, I will make sure you no longer have a job." Ida's lips tightened and for a moment we feared it hadn't worked and Anna would have had to follow through with her threat. Ida finally moved to one side, but it was too late. By the time we reached Missus Edith's room, the door was wide open and Elisabeth was safely in her mother's arms, retelling the entire event in between sobs that could only have been faked for effect.

Anna and I stood frozen in the doorway. The more Elisabeth told, the narrower Edith's glare became in our direction.

By the time Elisabeth had finished her tale, which turned out to involve me threatening her and trying to hurt her, and a scuffle that had Elisabeth as the hero, pinning me to the floor, Missus Edith was seething.

Anna rushed into the room, desperate to calm the situation. "Ruth was retrieving something for my father, that is all." But it only made things worse.

"Are you calling my daughter a liar?" Missus Edith shouted.

Anna shook her head, horrified. "No, I am saying my sister was given permission to be there."

"And what of the threats and the scuffle; was she given permission to do that too?"

Anna opened her mouth, then closed it again, as even she had realized the trap she was in. We both knew that to say the scuffle had never happened was to call Elisabeth a liar and Missus Edith would have found it easier to accept that Ruth had stolen the very jewellery around her neck without her knowing than to accept her daughter had lied.

"You!" Missus Edith pointed at me, shaking with rage. "You will be on the next ship back to where you came from and I will make sure cousin Walter is waiting for you at the port."

I felt my heart fall to my feet. Anna begged her to reconsider; she threw herself at Missus Edith's feet, grabbing on to the tail of her gown. "I will do anything," she pleaded, tears streaming down her face. "What do you want me to do? I will serve you. I will wait on you hand and foot. Please!" Her voice became hoarse from crying but it did no good.

I was still frozen in the doorway, watching my sister bargain for my life, my own face soaked, eyes so filled with tears I could barely see.

"I won't do it again," I promised, though my voice barely rose over my sister's own cries.

"I won't do it again," I repeated and I could barely swallow, my throat hurt so much. This was what I wanted, to go home, but not like that. Not without Anna, and not with Walter waiting. He would have me at an auction before the sun set.

Anna pulled herself up to her feet.

"I will tell Papa," she cried. "He won't let you."

But Missus Edith only sneered. "John cannot control what happens here when he leaves and he will not be here for ever."

Anna ran out of the door and down the stairs, and I followed her. We barged into the room where Master John had asked to be left alone and he was not too pleased to see us until he saw Anna was in tears. His annoyance changed to concern.

"Whatever has happened?" he asked, and Anna let go of my hand to wrap her arms around her father. The words spilled out in a tumble and none of it made any sense. Master John told her to calm down but didn't seem to notice or care that I was just as distressed.

Back home, it would have been Mama we ran to. She would have taken us both in her arms. I hugged myself, shivering alone while Anna was comforted.

"She is upset because Elisabeth will no longer play with her," Missus Edith said, entering the room, Elisabeth still wrapped around her.

"No," Anna said, between sobs, "she wants to send Ruth back, but she can't go back, can she, Papa, because she is not safe."

Master John stroked Anna's hair and looked at his sister, eyebrows raised. "Is that true, Edith?"

Missus Edith laughed hollowly, "Of course not; she's making up stories to get your attention, John."

"She did say it," I said, echoing my sister. "She said I was going back on the first ship."

Master John sighed at his sister. "I know I have asked a lot of you, Edith, but you cannot send them back when it gets too hard for you."

Missus Edith stroked her daughter's hair and nodded. "I know, and I would never do that. I gave you my word that they would be safe with me." I glared at her in disbelief at the lies coming out of her mouth with such ease.

"Good," Master John said, returning to his chair. He glanced at his pocket watch. "Now, I still have fifteen minutes of my time left, so sort this out between you."

"But, Papa," Anna attempted, but Master John waved her away. "That is enough, Anna."

We followed Missus Edith out, closing the door behind us. In the hallway, she turned on us, her smile fading.

119

"The second Jonathan leaves, *you*," she pointed at me, "will go back to the basement where you belong and that little performance has cost you two suppers. And believe me when I say that you *will* be on a boat back to that hellish place where you belong, one way or another. This other nuisance might be blood, but you are not. And it wont be long before Jonathan grows tired of your antics. Once he sees the money made from your sale, you will be all but forgotten."

She turned to Anna, "And don't you ever try to turn my brother against me again, or you will be next."

She led her daughter back up the stairs, her eyes never leaving us until she was out of sight.

Even when they were long gone, Anna and I stood frozen to the spot, clutching each other.

"What will we do, Ruth?" Anna whispered.

"We go to the tavern," I told her urgently. "The one with the people who are like us — who look like me. Francis says they can do anything, so maybe they can help us?"

There was a moment of silence from Anna as she sniffed away tears. She nodded slowly. "All right, yes, we should do that."

I closed my eyes, sighing with relief. Finally, Anna was on my side.

13.

ANNA

The footman was unwilling to take us without permission from the lady of the house or the gentleman, so Ruth prepared me on what to say to Papa. We stood outside the closed door watching the grandfather clock in the hall, the long hand moving slowly round until it reached the hour we were waiting for. It seemed to take for ever but eventually it boomed throughout the house and Ruth wasted no time pushing me through the door.

Papa was folding his newspaper away when I burst into the room, Ruth close behind me. He raised an eyebrow irritably. "What is it now?"

"It's Master Samuel Johnson," I said, speaking quickly before I lost my nerve. "He has sent word asking if you will join him this evening."

Papa frowned. He checked his watch. "It's a little short notice. When did this word arrive?"

I searched for my sister's hand and she slipped her fingers into mine as though she had been waiting; as though she knew that was what I would need.

I was never good at lying. Like anything that involved talking, I stumbled over my words.

"Only ten minutes ago," Ruth spoke up. "You asked not to be disturbed, so I took the message for you."

Papa thought about this for some minutes, then glanced at his watch. "I suppose I could spare an hour or two."

Ruth squeezed my hand but we didn't look at each other and we tried our hardest not to look too excited.

"All right," he said, standing with a grunt, "to Samuel's it is." As he walked by us, Ruth nudged me. I took a deep breath and summoned all my courage.

"Papa?"

He sighed, "Yes, Anna?"

"Can we come? Ruth and I?" I rushed through the words before he could say no. "We haven't been outside since we got here, we haven't even seen any of London, and Francis, the gentleman who came with Samuel, he invited us to see him. We would not get in your way, we promise. In fact, you would not even remember we were there."

I held my breath and I thought I might pass out for how long it took him to respond.

He looked at me, considering. "I could use some help carrying some things I would like to take along, though I am not sure I require both of you—" He must have noticed the expression on my face because he quickly said, "Very well. Ruth, collect my trunk from the office; it contains some very important papers so do be careful. Anna, you may help her and then both meet me outside at the carriage immediately."

He turned to shrug on his coat and marched out of the door.

Neither Ruth nor I could decide what we were more excited about: leaving Missus Edith's terrible house, seeing London in the daytime with all its sights, or meeting Francis again.

For the first time since we arrived in England, we put on our coats and hats. I hugged the cloth which is too thin for the English weather tightly, reminded suddenly of home.

"It smells like Mama," Ruth whispered, holding the collar of her coat to her nose. I nodded in agreement: it did smell like Mama.

Outside, London was grey and dismal, but it did nothing to dampen our spirits. Leaving the house took a heavy weight off my shoulders; suddenly I didn't feel like I had to pretend any more.

I sat by the right window across from Papa and Ruth sat to the left. I stuck my head out of the carriage window, gawping at all the sights and sounds.

The cobbled streets as the wheels of the carriage rolled over each stone. The stench of sewage. Women wearing beautiful gowns and extravagant hats despite the grey sky. Children with dirty faces by themselves, wearing torn clothes, begging on the street. Others being led around by nannies. Carriages going in both directions. The sound of hooves against the ground echoing into the carriage.

I looked over and smiled at how happy Ruth was. I hadn't seen her smile since we played chase in the fields back home. I sighed at the pretty dresses in the shop windows; if only that moment could have lasted for ever. If only we could have driven round and round in a never-ending loop, so we never had to stop and face the world ever again.

Papa pointed to the occasional landmark, or certain streets and who they were named after. The places he went to with his own father. Ruth slid over so she could also hear the stories, leaning her head against my shoulder. She tried a few times to ask Papa questions about what games he played, and where he went to school. But Papa either ignored her questions or snapped, "I'm talking."

Suddenly, the mood changed and Ruth slumped into her corner, folding her arms and pouting. I reached for her, but she shrugged me off.

"Look, Anna," Papa said, pointing out of the window, "see that store? My father owned it once, but the area has completely changed. I used to play in a field just around the corner." He chuckled, completely unaware that he had hurt Ruth's feelings.

It was only when the carriage stopped in a courtyard and the footman announced we had arrived that Ruth perked up.

She threw the door open, not waiting for the footman to open it for us, and landed feet first on the pebbled ground. I followed her, jumping from the carriage.

"Anna," Papa said disapprovingly.

I slinked back to his side as Ruth ran off shouting, "Which one?"

The carriage was outside a large black-and-white-stoned house. It had its own courtyard and a walkway leading around the back. On the other side, were more houses that looked the same as Papa's.

Despite Papa telling Ruth to wait, she ignored him and raced up the steps of the house. By the time Papa and I had reached her, she had already banged on the door three times.

Papa grabbed her hand as she went for another knock. "Three is enough to wake the dead," he snapped.

I felt her deflate beside me and I grabbed her hand in an attempt to comfort her. Despite Papa's words, I knew she was just excited. To be away from Missus Edith and Elisabeth was just what we both needed, but to be seeing Francis again felt a little bit like home. Finally, we would not feel like the odd ones out.

The door eventually opened and Francis stood on the threshold, looking out at us blankly.

"Mr Ambrose," he said, surprised. Ruth tried to grab his attention with her eyes. She moved her eyebrows up and down while darting her eyes in Papa's direction.

Francis noticed but frowned in confusion.

Papa gave him a short nod. "May we come in or will you make us stand out here all evening?"

Francis gathered himself, apologizing profusely while allowing us in. He took our coats, hanging them on the hooks on the wall.

"Are we early or late?" Papa asked. "The girls forgot to get a time from you."

Francis looked baffled again. "From me?" he asked.

I looked at him earnestly, begging him to save us.

"Yes, when you came round earlier with the invitation."

Francis stared at Papa as if waiting for more, but he got

nothing. "The invitation..." Francis said slowly, his eyes darting back and forth as if beseeching his brain to fill in the blanks.

"For tea," I offered, stepping forward so Papa couldn't see the pleading in my eyes. We couldn't possibly have come this far only to fail. "You came around and said Master Samuel had invited Papa for tea, but I forgot to ask you for a time because you were in such a rush." When he still didn't get it, I tried again, more earnest this time. "We so desperately wanted to see you again, my sister and I." I pulled Ruth beside me and she fixed her eyes on him.

Slowly, the light came on behind his eyes. Whether it was our desperate faces, begging him to go along with our story, or he had convinced himself he really had brought an invitation to the house, I couldn't tell.

"Ah," he said, striking a finger in the air, "yes, yes." He rushed past an impatient Papa, knocking on the first door on the left. A voice boomed for him to enter and he did, closing the door quickly behind him, much to Papa's annoyance.

Ruth looked at me gleefully and I couldn't help but fill with pride.

As we waited, we looked around us. Master Samuel Johnson's house was not as grand as Papa's, despite the look on the outside. The hallway was a small dark space with only two wooden chairs against a wall. The stairs leading upstairs looked much the same as Edith's, dark wood, but they felt much different. Unlike Edith's house where everything was organized and people worked quietly so as not to disturb her, here it was as busy as the streets outside. Faces appeared up and down the hall, in and out of rooms, and it was hard to tell who was visiting and who lived there. Most looked poor, some ill, but no one seemed to pay them any mind.

"Samuel takes in the poor and the sick," Papa explained as a young man hobbled by us, holding his stomach. Papa shook his head as if in disapproval. "He does not seem to understand he cannot save everyone."

There was lots of chatter upstairs, the clatter of dishes downstairs and the smell of soup wafted up. It was chaotic, but so much more homely than Edith's house, so much more like home.

No one was tiptoeing in the hopes of not upsetting the owner; everyone seemed relaxed and no one seemed dressed like an uppity lady or a gentleman.

The door reopened and Francis stepped out. "My apologies for keeping you waiting," he said, gesturing for us to enter. The room had a huge fireplace on the opposite wall from the door that drowned the tiny room. Paintings of men in grey wigs adorned the green-painted walls. There was not much else except a few chairs around a dark wooden table and one long window with curtains shielding the people inside from the outside.

Samuel got to his feet and shook Papa's hand. He towered over him like a giant, wearing a white wig that had seen better days. His clothes were the same as when we saw him last, ill-fitting and in need of a good wash. Ruth and I hung back nervously. Every time anyone spoke I caught my breath, thinking we would be found out. For a second there was an awkward silence, then Master Samuel broke it with a smile. "It is good to see you again so soon. Sit, sit."

I let out an audible sigh of relief that we had got away with it, temporarily, but there was still the rest of the evening and who knew where the conversation would go.

Master Samuel asked Francis to bring his favourite port and Francis obliged. He beckoned me and Ruth to join him to fetch it.

We followed him along the hall and down narrow winding stairs, just like the ones in Edith's house. Francis warned us to be careful; the wooden floor could be slippery from spilt gravy.

"Little Peter can be very clumsy," he said, chuckling.

When we reached the bottom floor, the kitchen was a hub of activity. Unlike Edith's house there was laughter and chatter and no one seemed to be shouting. Francis ruffled the hair of a young boy sitting on a stool.

"You haven't spilled anything on the stairs, have you, Peter?"

The boy shook his head proudly. "No, sir."

Francis invited us to sit at the long wooden table. He manoeuvred around the cook and her assistant to a cupboard where he pulled out a dark bottle that looked very much like the port Papa drank.

"So," Francis said, placing two small glasses on a tray and the bottle beside it. "What is the real reason you have duped Mr Ambrose into bringing you here?"

So, he did realize what we were doing after all. I beamed and started to tell him the entire story, constantly interrupted by Ruth as she took over. We spoke quickly, desperate to get it all out before Papa came to find us.

When we eventually finished, Francis looked at us both solemnly.

"And what is it you would like to ask of me?" he asked finally.

"Take us to the tavern!" Ruth blurted out. "You said there are people like us. Maybe they will know what to do?"

"Because you believe I alone won't know what to do?" he asked, hand on his chest.

"No," I said quickly, panicking that we may have caused offence, "not at all."

There was a small twinkle in his eye, and he smiled as he said, "Follow me."

We followed him back up the winding stairs, along the hall and into the room where Papa and Master Samuel sat at a small round table, eating dinner the maid had served them. Francis placed the glasses in front of them and the bottle in the middle of the table.

"Won't you join us, Francis?" Samuel asked, as Francis turned to leave.

Francis gave a short nod of appreciation. "If Mr Ambrose doesn't mind, I am thinking of taking the girls for a walk while you both catch up. I know there is much for you two to discuss that maybe would not be . . . suitable for such young ears."

Ruth gripped my arm in excitement.

Papa didn't look very sure.

I crossed my fingers behind my back, willing Papa to say yes.

He turned to Samuel who smiled pleasantly.

"I am sure you both could use some fresh air and Francis knows the cobbled streets of London like the back of his hand."

Papa nodded with some reluctance and I ran over to him and hugged him tightly. "Thank you, Papa," I whispered. He patted my arm before telling us to be on our way.

Excitedly, we followed Francis back into the hall and I couldn't stop talking, I was so excited.

"Will it be busy? How many people will be there? What exactly do they do there? And where are they all from?"

Francis answered each of my questions patiently as he led us outside into the same courtyard we had arrived in earlier. I waited on the curb for him to call the footman but he didn't. Instead, Francis fixed his hat, adjusted his jacket and stepped into the road. So we followed, curious for this adventure.

"You know you have a unique relationship with Mr Ambrose," he observed, moving on to the pavement. "It is very unusual for a slave owner to bring two slave girls to England for their own benefit. Usually, slaves are brought here because the owner cannot bear to be without the service he has become accustomed to."

"My sister is not a slave," Ruth said as I linked arms with Francis. I leaned forward to glare at her, knowing she was about to ruin the evening. "She is more…" Ruth paused to think, a finger under her chin, "…she is more an acquaintance of servantry."

The words sounded clunky in her mouth, like something she had heard once and was repeating but did not fully comprehend. This only made me wonder where she had heard it.

Francis laughed politely but I didn't find it funny. Ruth was trying to say I wasn't the same as her.

"Yet here we both are," I said airily so as not to show myself up in front of Francis, "in the same predicament."

Ruth shot me a look and I stuck my chin in the air, ready to defend myself. It was not often that I stood up to Ruth, and it felt good.

Francis raised a hand between us. "Girls, girls. We are all slaves. Whether we are inside the house or out in the fields, and whether our skin is dark as night or pale as dawn. They see us all the same."

"But now Missus Edith wants to send me back," Ruth mumbled, "and she says she will make sure the overseer is there to meet me."

"Can she do that?" I asked Francis worriedly.

We came to the end of the courtyard and turned on to a bigger and wider road filled with carriages travelling in both directions. The sound of hooves thundered in our ears and Francis had to shout over the noise.

"Missus Edith's ways are not unique," Francis said. "You will find that most of the wealthy are exactly the same. That is why they all get along so well."

Two older women walked by us and Francis moved out of the way, tipping his hat, but they paid him no mind. In fact, they seemed quite offended that he should even acknowledge them. Francis picked up pace and had us almost running to keep up with him.

"It is not good to be seen wandering around the streets of London after dark," he mumbled, more to himself than to anyone else. "Not for us."

I instinctively huddled closer to him.

We turned down a dark alleyway between two large buildings. I grabbed his arm nervously and Ruth must have felt the same because she grabbed his other arm as he led us along the cobbled path that he seemed to know so well.

Eventually he stopped outside a small wooden door that could lead anywhere, with the words *Fleet Street Tavern* carved above it.

Francis knocked in a pattern of six counts. Seconds later, a scraping sound as a piece of wood was pulled back, revealing a square opening at the top of the door. A pair of eyes looked out and assessed us before closing the window.

A few seconds later the door was opened and music escaped on to the cobbled street.

14.

RUTH

A black man, not much taller than Francis but with wide shoulders and thicker arms, broke into a gap-toothed smile. They exchanged pleasantries before Francis turned to introduce me and Anna.

"Just arrived from Jamaica," he told the stranger.

He looked us over. "Slaves?"

Francis nodded. The stranger frowned, and raised his eyebrows in Anna's direction as if to ask, *"Even this one?"* It was a look that Ruth had seen directed at her sister several times.

Francis changed the subject quickly. "We are in need of some counsel. May we come in?"

The stranger draped his arm over Francis's shoulder and led him inside. "You are always welcome here,

Francis. This place is for us all."

We followed the two men cautiously along a dark wooden corridor where only one person could walk at a time. The music got louder the further in we got until we entered a room at the end of the hall filled with candles, tables and people. People who looked like us. Different shapes, shades and sizes, men, women, girls and boys. About forty of them were crammed into the low-ceilinged room.

Anna grabbed my hand and I accepted it as we both looked around us in bewilderment.

In the far corner, a man with greased-down hair and a thick beard served drinks behind a counter. To the right of the counter, on a small stage, five men and women were playing instruments while people danced in the small space between the stage and the tables. There was whooping and cheering and clapping to the beat. Dark wooden tables with matching chairs were occupied by groups of people, some animated by laughter, some by deep discussion.

"It's ... like ... home," I breathed in disbelief. And I didn't mean the plantation, not at all. Rather the sense of home one felt when wrapped up in their mama's arms, or lost in a story with a dear sister, or surrounded by loved ones under a starry night sky.

Home.

Francis came back to get us as we stood in the doorway.

"Welcome," he said. "This is home."

I suddenly felt like I was with family once more.

Something about the tavern felt so familiar. It wasn't just the fact that everyone in the room looked like us. It was the cackle from someone at a table, hitting his knees with laughter as the woman next to him whispered in his ear. It was the sheer joy on the faces of those dancing, as though they had just been released from something painful, and they were so grateful to be there. The smiles were contagious and immediately Anna was grabbed by a lady who swung her around the room to the music.

Anna reached for me to join in, because Anna always was uncomfortable dancing, but Francis tapped me on the shoulder.

"Come," he said, and he led me over to a table with three men and a woman and a girl.

Francis leaned on the table and spoke to them in a low tone. I didn't know how they could hear anything he was saying over the music. He beckoned to me. A young girl, probably only a few years older than me, pulled out a seat. All eyes were on me as I sat down.

"Tell them," he said, "tell them everything."

So I told them about Jamaica. About Mama and about Master John. I told them about Walter the overseer and what happened the day we were playing chase through the plantation. They shook their heads when I told them about

Sarah; how I tried to stop her from a lashing and how that made the overseer mad.

Without me realizing it, more people had gathered around the table, who called more people until the music stopped and the entire room was listening. The walls echoed with tuts as I relayed the overseer's threats.

Familiarity filled their faces and they exchanged looks I couldn't read when I told them how Mama begged Master John to save us.

The quieter the room became, the more my voice filled the space. I told them about Missus Edith, and a murmur swept through the room as though she was well known among them.

Or maybe, like Francis said, they all had an Edith. Her behaviour was familiar to them – it was the behaviour of the women who had passed us on the street, refusing to acknowledge Francis's greeting, and countless others.

I told them about the parties, about the library and finally, Missus Edith's threat to send me back. I had no doubt that she would wait for Master John's anger to settle, for him to be off on business yet again, before going through with her plan. Of course, he would be angry at her for disobeying his orders, but as long as Walter fetched a pretty price, I didn't believe he would miss me at all. Deep down, I knew that Master John had never cared for me, and never would, despite Anna's beliefs. Everything he did, he did for Anna and sometimes Mama. Anna was his daughter and maybe he truly cared for Mama.

But at the end of the day, I was still just a slave. His property.

When I had finished, the room erupted into loud chatter and I couldn't make out if what they were saying was good or bad.

"This is nothing new," one man shouted over the noise. "This happens. This is our life. It will always be our life. So, what do you expect us to do?"

The room quietened again as some avoided my eyes. Francis rested his arm on my shoulder and it was comforting.

"Just because it happens often, George, does not mean we turn a blind eye and do nothing when it does. We have only each other." He looked around the room at everyone. "We cannot allow this child to be sent to her death. Or it will no longer be on the hands of others, but it will be on us too." He squeezed my shoulder. "We must do something."

"But what?" someone else shouted. "What can we do?"

Francis sighed, shrugging his shoulders. "That is why we are here. They asked to see you. We are a room filled with servants of doctors and judges, of skilled men and women, sailors, poets and musicians.

Can we not put together one idea?"

The room fell silent as everyone thought long and hard.

"When is she sending you away?" the girl next to me asked.

"When Master John leaves," I replied.

"And when is that?"

I realized then that I didn't know when Master John was leaving and I felt a little silly in front of all these people.

"In two days," a small voice replied. Everyone turned to where the voice was coming from and it was Anna, standing by the door, looking completely terrified of the attention.

For a moment, I had forgotten she was here.

"All right," one of them said, nodding his head slowly. "So, we have two days."

"No," Francis said, "he *leaves* in two days, so we have *one*."

Half-formed ideas were thrown back and forth between the group; some were immediately shot down, others were put to one side, but after an hour, Francis said he had to take us back.

Albert, the man who had opened the door to us earlier, patted him on the back. "We will find a way."

As we followed him out of the room and towards the door, I plucked up the courage to ask, "What do we do until then?" I was frantic at the idea of returning to Missus Edith's.

Albert smiled at me gently, "Wait for our instructions. We will be in touch soon."

When we returned, Master John was waiting outside the carriage. Francis apologized for keeping him waiting. "It is not your fault, Francis," he said, "I have had some urgent news, that is all."

"Nothing too serious, I hope?" Francis enquired. Master John sighed.

"I cannot be sure. We shall see," he replied.

He beckoned for me and Anna to get in the carriage; before we did, we wrapped our arms around Francis so tightly it surprised Master John.

"What have you done to them?" he asked, bemused but with a slight edge in his voice. Sensing Master John's change in tone, Francis replied cheerfully that we had enjoyed seeing the sights nearby, that was all.

I climbed into the carriage feeling hopeful. The horse pulled us along in silence except for the sound of its hooves and I became lost in my thoughts, remembering all the ideas the men and women in the tavern had come up with to save us. I felt warm and fuzzy, recalling the room with all the people who looked just like me, and my heart sang for the first time since leaving Mama.

When we returned to the house it was late and Master

John told us he had lots to do. He disappeared upstairs to his room. I said goodnight to Anna and tiptoed downstairs and into the corner I shared with Mary. As I slipped under the thin blanket, Mary raised herself up by her elbows.

"Where have you been? The missus is not happy." But nothing could stop my joy.

Not even evil Missus Edith.

I rolled over on to my side, turning away from Mary, and murmured, "I had the best night I have ever had since I came here, Mary."

"What did you do?" She asked curiously, but I didn't answer.

Instead, I closed my eyes, trying to remember every detail of the night. The leaning building, the name above that wasn't straight. The dark narrow walkway with walls that closed in on you then opened into a bright room with laughter and music. I tried to remember the faces: the young girl with the warm smile, her hair pulled back with a part in the middle, who offered me a chair. The man across from her who led the conversation, the dancing, the music. It was all so normal, so freeing, so much like home when the overseer had left, and Master John was away, and Mama took us to where the field slaves stayed. The fire that was lit in the centre of all the huts. Old man Don with his singing, and the kitchen ladies beating the back of pans for drums. We shared food and laughter.

The adults sharing stories passed from generation to generation, of a time even the greying adults were too young to remember. A time before slavery. The kids playing games in the dirt, chasing each other around the fire until they fell in a pile on top of each other.

When we returned to the house at the end of the night and I had told Mama how perfect those nights were, she had replied, "It's not perfect, Ruth; it is surviving."

Maybe, I thought as my eyes grew heavy, *maybe I could survive in this country, if surviving meant I could go to the tavern every day.*

When I next woke it was with a jolt. My body hit cold ground and then I was hauled to my feet but my feet were still asleep.

I gasped awake to hear Mary asking, "What are you doing to her?" but it was too dark to see, and my eyes wouldn't adjust quick enough no matter how many times I squeezed them closed then opened them again.

Someone big grunted – a man, I knew that much. I smelled sweat and horse manure. He grabbed me by the waist and carried me under his arm like a sack of flour.

Something was wrong.

He marched through the kitchen where I caught a glimpse of Ida in her nightgown, a candle in her hand.

Then we were going up the winding stairs to the first floor and that was when I started kicking and screaming. The man grunted in annoyance. His arms were large and he wore a musky brown coat that smelled of cigars.

Somehow, we reached the top of the stairs. I let out a bellowing scream that was sure to wake the household. I struggled under the stranger's hold, but it was firm and he didn't flinch. The front door was wide open, and even from this distance, I could see a dark figure waiting beside a carriage.

I panicked, trying as hard as I could to slip out of his grasp, when Missus Edith appeared in front of me, grinning from ear to ear.

She opened her mouth to say something but was interrupted by a shrill scream and the sound of soft feet rushing down the stairs. Anna. She ran to me, grabbing my hands, and it was the energy I needed to fight.

"No, no, no!" Anna cried frantically. She turned to Missus Edith, "Stop it. Please, stop him."

But Missus Edith's grin only grew wider. "I told you this would happen, did I not?"

My heart dropped to the pit of my stomach as I realized what was happening.

"Anna," I wept, but no other words came out. I was paralysed by fear. Anna ran to block the stranger's path while screaming her father's name repeatedly until her voice hoarse.

"He's gone," Missus Edith shouted over her. "Not long after you came home from your trip. He has business in Liverpool and then he is taking a ship straight back. Not to worry, I'll have your friend waiting at the port for you long before Jonathan arrives."

We stared at her in disbelief. For a moment, there was stunned silence as we realized we had run out of time. I would be gone before Francis and the others could even form a plan. How naïve we had been!

The man tried to step around Anna, who was still in his way, while still clutching on to me, but again she blocked his path.

"No!" Her voice was filled with sheer terror.

She grabbed my hands again and we held on to each other for dear life.

But neither of us were a match for the burly man. He knocked Anna out of the way with barely a shove. Even as she fell to the ground, we didn't let go of each other. There was another scuffle as Anna wrapped herself around his legs while I pounded him with my fists.

"Ida," Missus Edith said. It was then that I noticed Ida had followed us upstairs and was standing nearby. At the sound of her name, she set the candle down and grabbed hold of Anna, prying her from the man's legs and holding her down.

I strained to see my sister desperately trying to climb out from under Ida's weight.

"I'll find you," Anna screamed before Missus Edith triumphantly slammed the door shut.

15.

ANNA

I lay on the floor bawling into the ground, my throat sore, but the tears wouldn't stop. My heart ached in ways I never imagined it would. I saw no further than that moment. I was torn from my sister and I had no idea where they had taken her. I screamed into my hands.

I didn't hear or see Edith, Ida and the rest of the household return to their beds. I didn't hear them shut their doors to block me out. All I could think about was Mama. How I had failed her. The only thing she asked was that we looked after each other. Ruth had always kept me safe, and now she was gone. I rolled about on the floor, holding my belly because the pain was unbearable.

"Anna, please," Elisabeth begged. She got down on her knees and tried to take my hand, but I shrugged her off. I hated it here. I hated everyone in this house and I especially hated this girl trying to act concerned when it was most likely her mouth that had got us to this point.

"Please, Anna. Do you want hot chocolate? I can get the cook to make us some. It will make you feel better."

I wished she would go away and leave me alone. The very sound of her voice was making me worse.

"How about you wear my favourite dress?" she suggested excitedly. "The one you love so much. I'll let you wear it for a whole week."

I turned on to my side to look at her through bloodshot eyes. "I hate that dress," I told her through sniffles and a croaky voice. "I only tell you I love it so you will let me see my sister. It's hideous and makes you look like a cake."

I broke down again at the very word 'sister'.

When my tears finally slowed, I sat up and noticed I was alone. Elisabeth had gone.

I crawled over to the banister and slowly pulled myself up on to my feet. I climbed the stairs, one step at a time, my body weak from the tussle in the hall, my eyes stinging from crying. When I reached my room, I closed the door and slumped on the bed with its patterned covers and matching curtains. There was a rocking chair in the corner of the room that always seemed to rock by itself, as it did now. As if someone invisible sat there.

I wanted so much to tell Ruth about the mystery rocking chair, but I never got the chance because every time I had seen my sister something had happened. I rolled on to my side and stared at the rocking chair until the hiccups subsided. I thought of my sister screaming, the look in her eyes as she was taken out of the house and my promise to find her.

I sighed a deep and long sigh. I wasn't brave, not like my sister. I wanted so much to be as brave as her. To protect others even if it meant putting myself in danger the way she always did. The problem was, I was too afraid of the consequences. I didn't want to make things worse for anyone, especially for Mama and Ruth.

I remembered Mama telling me to look out for Ruth. I knew what that meant, even though she had never said the words out loud. I had something my sister and our mother never had. I was not a threat.

It was not just the colour of my skin. Mama had taught me how to smile, to lower my eyes to the ground. To laugh when they laughed; to be attentive and obedient. I was to make them believe how grateful

I was to be in the circle, and I would not let them down.

The thought went round and round in my head until suddenly something clicked. I pulled myself up to sitting.

I am in the circle. For now. Tomorrow I might not be. But tonight, I am.

I took a deep breath and wiped my eyes and nose with the back of my hand. I slid off the bed and walked over to the wooden wardrobe. I opened it and picked out a simple black dress with a high collar, one that would be easy to move in. My fingers were shaking as I buttoned it all the way to the top. I combed my hair in a daze, pinning it up with as many pins as I could find. I paused and looked at myself in the vanity mirror. "Anna, you can do this," I mumbled over and over until I had enough courage.

I opened the bedroom door. The house was silent as if nothing had ever happened. There were no signs that Ruth was gone. No sad music, no tears from anyone, no echoes of her screams still lingering.

I steadied my breath and knocked on Elisabeth's bedroom door.

"Anna, you can do this." I continued to repeat the words over and over. No one answered from the other side, so I opened the door softly and peered in. The room was dark, but I could see a large shape under all the covers.

I tiptoed over to the bed and leaned in to see if she was sleeping.

"I'm not sleeping," Elisabeth said, annoyed. She raised her head out of the covers and I could just about make out she was still upset.

"Will you lend me that dress?" I asked softly, running my fingers against the covers.

She scowled. "You said you hated it."

I avoided her eyes. "I was upset, but really I do want to borrow it; it looks so beautiful on you. You look like a princess in it."

Elisabeth sat up and looked at me. "You really think so?"

I nodded, finally looking her in the eye, attentive, telling her what she wanted to hear. "I've never seen anyone look more beautiful than you," I said, twisting my fingers into my dress so she couldn't see my nerves.

Elisabeth broke into a smile, tucking her hair behind her ears. "All right. I forgive you for being so rude to me." She took my shaking hand in hers. "And I promise I won't let Mother punish you."

I forced a smile. The one that told them I was not a threat. I was just a simple girl, grateful to be in the circle. "I'm so grateful to you, Elisabeth, but I do need a favour from you." I squeezed her hand in mine. "As my best friend, I have only you to turn to."

Elisabeth leaned in conspiratorially. "What is it, Anna?"

We crept downstairs, trying to avoid the creaks in the wooden floor that might wake the house. Elisabeth held on to me so tightly her grip pinched my skin. I bit my lip but said nothing.

"This is not like me at all," she whispered anxiously. "I never lie to Mother." We reached the bottom of the stairs and I turned to face her. I still did not trust Elisabeth, but she was all I had.

"You are doing it for her, remember? Did you call on the footman?"

She nodded. "He will be waiting outside and he knows where to go." She was quiet for a moment, lost in thought. "So, you have a present for Mother but you left it at Mr Johnson's house?"

I nodded firmly, crossing my fingers behind my back.

"But why can't you go get it when it is light?"

"Because your mother sees everything," I explained, glancing at the clock in the corner of the hall. "I couldn't possibly hide it from her during the day, and then the surprise would be ruined. If I go now, then I can be back and have it waiting for her for when she wakes."

I pulled on my coat and opened the front door cautiously.

"But won't Mr Johnson be upset that you woke him?"

I shook my head confidently even though I had the same worry myself. "No, I won't wake him. I will wake his servant, Francis. I will knock on the back door."

I rushed towards the carriage where the footman was waiting, before Elisabeth changed her mind, or worse still, Edith woke up.

The footman opened the carriage door and I climbed in. I leaned out of the window and waved to Elisabeth, who stood in the doorway with her arms wrapped around herself. I felt a pang of guilt, watching her shiver in her nightgown.

"You will come back, won't you, Anna?" she asked. I pretended not to hear her, waving enthusiastically while the horse trotted away. When she was no longer in sight, I slumped into the darkness of the carriage and let out a deep sigh of relief, which slowly turned to hysterical tears.

As we rode along the quiet London streets, I realized through hiccups that I had never been alone like this. Ruth was always somewhere close, and it had been a constant comfort knowing she was never very far.

I twisted my fingers in my lap, biting the skin on my

lip, checking the window every few seconds to make sure we were going in the right direction and Elisabeth hadn't tricked me.

The truth was, I wouldn't have known even if the driver had gone the wrong way. London was so big and I had only seen glimpses through a carriage window.

Never in the dark like this.

The carriage came to a slow stop, then silence. I waited for the door to open but nothing ... so cautiously I opened the door myself and stepped out on to the pavement.

I peered up at the footman who had not moved.

"Thank you, sir. You can go now," I told him in my most confident voice.

He looked down at me, expressionless. "Miss Elisabeth instructed me to wait."

I closed my eyes momentarily to calm my nerves as I realized I hadn't anticipated Elisabeth using the driver as a spy. I decided this was the least of my worries and hurried to the front door of Master Samuel's house, wondering how to wake Francis. I considered trying to call his name. Or knocking softly, or going around the back to try one of the other staff who could still have been awake.

But then I thought about what it would look like for someone to find me outside the servants' door in the middle of the night, and the complications that would come with that. So I banged on the door as hard and as loud as my knuckles allowed.

The door was finally opened by a dishevelled Francis, who had to blink twice before realizing who was standing in front of him.

"Anna?"

A tumble of words and tears spilled out as I tried to retell the events of the night. Saying the words out loud only sent me into hysterical tears again and Francis tried to calm me, saying he couldn't understand what I was saying.

He ushered me inside and the house was even darker than before. The housemaid had risen to enquire about the noise along with other servants, but Francis sent them back to bed, telling them there was nothing to worry about. One woman, though, refused to retire. She demanded to know who had disturbed the house at this ungodly hour.

Francis drew in a frustrated breath. "Miss Jane," he said with a clenched jaw, "it is not your concern, so I kindly ask you to return to your room." Miss Jane, the woman in a long white nightgown and a nightcap, scowled, getting ready to continue the argument, but Francis ushered me into the parlour and lit a candle so we could see each other.

He sat me down at the table. "Goodness, you are

shaking," he said, and disappeared from the room, telling me he would be back soon. Outside the door I could hear raised voices between Miss Jane and Francis, then silence.

I sat at the edge of the seat under the candlelight, twisting my fingers nervously in my lap, sniffing back the tears.

Minutes later, Francis returned with hot tea and placed it in my shaking hands. "Drink up," he whispered, "it will calm your nerves."

I obliged and drank the tea as quickly as I could, suddenly aware from the grandfather clock how late it was becoming. When I had finished, Francis took the cup and leaned forward in his chair.

"Now, tell me again, what has happened to make you so upset, dear Anna?"

It seemed to take for ever to retell the story. I kept forgetting bits, like Ida sitting on me or Ruth begging me to find her. But as soon as I finished everything went fast.

Francis told me to wait, and he disappeared again. When he returned, he was dressed and wearing his coat and hat.

"Come," he beckoned me. I jumped to my feet and followed him outside into the cold night. I linked arms with him as we rushed by the carriage and the driver still waiting. We hurried along the same street we had walked just the day before, this time without Ruth.

I immediately knew where we were going.

When Francis knocked on the door this time, he was as frantic as I was when I knocked on his. The usual eyes popped out to inspect, then the door opened and it was the same man from last time, Albert, looking pleasantly surprised to see Francis. But his smile soon vanished when he saw Francis's expression.

"Gather everyone," Francis said as we hurried along the dark corridor and into the room where softer music was playing and a woman wearing a head wrap and an extravagant gown sang to the room. Albert rushed to the front of the room and whispered something in the musicians' ears. They stopped playing immediately. Francis joined him and called for everyone's attention, while I hovered by the door, my fingers entwined against my dress. Francis told the room the story of how my sister Ruth was taken in the middle of the night.

To my surprise, no one laughed it off, or said it was none of their business. No one said, "This happens all the time." The response was quick as people shouted out ideas of what to do next, of splitting into groups, searching the area, but only one idea caught Francis's attention. A small quiet boy with short curly hair parted to the side had to speak a few times before he was heard over the room. Francis called him to the front and asked him to repeat what he had just said.

The boy, whose name was Bill, told them that, as a servant to Judge Barnabus, he knew that by law Ruth could not be forced back to the colonies. I caught my breath in disbelief. The hint of some hope was almost too much to think about.

"The law was changed after the Somerset case," he explained, looking directly at me. "A slave tried to run away but his master caught him and put him on a ship. Lucky for him, his godparents put a stop to it and the case was taken to court. There, the judge agreed that a master could not forcibly send a slave abroad."

"It was a great day for us all," Francis agreed, to murmurs around the room. "So," Francis prompted Bill, "how do we stop them?"

Bill thought about this for some time and I begged him under my breath to have the answer. "We ask the judge for a letter demanding her return," he said.

The room liked this idea, and everyone jumped to their feet but Francis shook his head. "We cannot all go descending on the judge's house; we will be arrested. Just a few of us will do."

"I want to come," a voice said, and I recognized the girl who was sitting next to Ruth earlier. Francis nodded and we all left together. There were five of us in all: Francis, me, Bella, Bill and Albert.

16.

RUTH

The bulky man who took me from my bed threw me
into the carriage and before I had time to pick myself up
off the floor, he was in the carriage blocking my path.
The woman got in, closed the door and sat the other
side of me so I was blocked in and the carriage took off.

I tried again to climb over them, but they were
quick and hauled me back into my seat.

"Don't be stupid," the man said in a gruff voice.

I sank back into the seat to catch my breath and it
was only then that I realized how much my body hurt.

I had not felt a thing inside the house when I had
tried to fight them off, but since I had stopped fighting,
all the feelings rushed inside me and I felt everything.
My breathing slowed but my heart did not.

I thought about my sister left alone in that house, and how we didn't even see this coming. Hot tears brimmed in my eyes and I tried to blink them back.

I told myself off for crying. *You don't have time for this, Ruth, think!* I glanced out of the window but it was pitch black.

"Where are we going?" I asked. Neither of them answered. This only made me angry and I waited for the carriage to slow as I knew it would need to at some point. It couldn't keep this pace for ever.

Sure enough it slowed and as I peered out of the dark window, I glimpsed a sudden source of light.

It can't be...

But it was. The tavern.

Without thinking, I leapt to my feet and threw myself at the door. The carriage started moving again and the door swung open with me hanging off it. From behind I felt someone grab me and I held on to the door handle for dear life.

The cobbled streets hovered below me and I thought about how this could be my last chance to escape, so I let go of the handle and braced for impact. I closed my eyes and thought about Mama, and her singing in the kitchen. I thought about Anna chasing me in the fields. Suddenly, I was hauled back into the carriage, the door slamming shut as I fell to the carriage floor. The woman stood over me, shouting, telling me I was a pain in the neck.

"If you don't sit still, I'll throw you out there myself," she said, yanking me to my feet before dropping me on the seat next to her friend.

I sank into the seat, the smell of the pair of them overwhelming me, their hands pinning mine down. The man took a rope out of his bag and wrapped my arms tight with it, then he wrapped the rest around his wrist to hold on to me.

There was nowhere for me to go and for some reason I felt almost relieved. I was so tired of fighting. I was tired of looking over my shoulder wondering when my time would come. Maybe it was time I accepted what was always destined for me: to go home without my sister. Mama would be distraught, but she would get over it, as would Anna. She would get over it and she would move on. At least this way, she could live her life without worrying about being my sister.

I felt my body start to shake as the tears came streaming down. I cried quietly, not wanting them to see or hear me. My chest hurt from the pain of never seeing my sister again, and no matter how much I tried, I couldn't stop the tears from falling.

Once I had accepted my fate, it was as if my body shut down. It no longer needed to fight. No longer needed to be on alert. The rocking of the carriage along the bumpy roads and the darkness outside eventually sent me to sleep.

When I woke, the carriage had stopped and the man was outside talking in a lowered voice to the driver. They both glanced at me before the man put money in the driver's hand. Minutes later the man walked around the carriage and disappeared.

The driver beckoned me out, "Come on."

I stood with my arms tied and manoeuvred out of the carriage. He helped me down and took the other end of the rope. He led me away from the carriage and it was only then that I realized we were not at the port. Instead we were at a tavern – not the *Fleet Street Tavern*, but one that I had never seen before. Soft candlelight came through the windows and occasionally I heard loud laughter.

The driver pulled me past the entrance of the tavern and towards a barn where he stopped to take the candle burning on the side and led me in. He moved the candle around to get his bearings and I saw the barn was filled with horses and manure. The stench was overwhelming and made me gag.

"Mister," I said quietly as he led me around the horses and to the back, "Mister, what they go do wi mi?"

He didn't answer. Instead he tied the rope around a wooden frame.

"Mister, please," I begged. "Have some mercy. They go send me home? To Jamaica?"

The man looked up from his tying. "They're sending you on a boat, yes," he replied before tightening the knot. He went to walk away but I put my hand out to stop him.

"Please help me," I begged, and I don't think he knew how hard that was to say. To ask the white man for help, when the white man had never helped me. He looked down at my hand and I pulled away quickly.

"Please," I begged again, and the tears started to fall once more. "I'll pay you. My sister, her father owns that house you took me from. She will make sure you're taken care of if you help me."

He looked at me and there was pity in his eyes but then it was gone. "I'm already being paid," he said, walking away, "and these people are not to be trifled with. It's not worth my life."

He disappeared into the night.

"I beg you," I screamed after him. "Please save me."

But only the horses heard me and they scuffled away from me. I continued to scream and shout and beg until my voice was hoarse and it was clear no one was coming to save me.

Finally, out of breath and weak, I slid on to the muddy ground and huddled against the post, resting my head against my hands. A dog appeared out of nowhere and sniffed me, then it lay down beside me with its head on my lap. For some reason this was the last straw. I began to sob, my body shaking like a leaf.

17.

ANNA

We rode in one carriage, with Albert as the driver. We closed the curtains of the carriage to avoid suspicion.

When we reached the judge's house, Francis told me to go in with Bill. "You must say Ruth is your servant," he instructed me. "She was stolen but a few hours ago and you would like a letter to have her returned."

I nodded nervously. Bella pulled my hat over my curls and smiled at me reassuringly. "Be yourself," she said, "he will believe you."

I forced a watery smile and wiped the tears away but Bella stopped me. "Keep the tears."

Bill, who was not much older than me, offered me his arm and led me into the quietness of the judge's house.

We climbed the stairs with walls filled with paintings of men wearing white wigs. Bill relayed information to me in a lowered tone. "He will be awake in his office. He rarely sleeps, but he will be tired and short-tempered." I looked at him, horrified. "Don't worry," Bill said, trying to reassure me. "He won't shout at you, not if he believes you are the same as him and that you are a lady."

We reached the top of the stairs and stood outside a room with a beam of yellow light spilling under the door. Bill looked at me and nodded. I took a deep breath, released my arm from his and smoothed my dress, then I gave him the nod.

He knocked on the door softly.

"Enter."

Bill opened the door and stepped in. "Master, you have a visitor." He turned to me and gave me a reassuring smile. I took a deep breath and stepped inside.

Under a dim lamp I moved into the room, my eyes lowered to the floor to not give too much of myself away. "I'm so sorry to disturb you, sir—" I began but I was immediately interrupted.

"A child? What business has a child at this time of night? Who do you belong to?"

It threw me a little but I continued despite his

questions. "My maidservant whom I have known all my life has been stolen in the middle of the night, to be sent back to the colonies, and I wondered, sir, if you could help me?"

There was a silence which forced me to look up.

He was staring at me, puzzled, "What family do you come from?"

I hesitated. Should I tell him the truth or lie? Surely, he couldn't know everyone in London. "The Ambroses," I said quietly.

He frowned, looking off into the distance, thinking. "Master John Ambrose?"

My heart fell. "Yes, sir, but my father is away on business and I was left with my maid as a companion, but she has been taken, to be forced on a ship and sent home."

He looked me over, squinting under the light, his face wrinkled and his dark eyes tired.

"I heard Master John had a child in Jamaica and he was bringing her home." He paused, rubbing his chin. "What happened to your mother?"

I knew Papa had not told anyone Mama was a slave, and neither had Missus Edith. It was an embarrassment neither of them wanted to face.

"She died in childbirth," I whispered, filled with overwhelming guilt. "I'm sorry, Mama,"

I whispered under my breath.

He seemed to accept this. "On whose orders was the slave sent away?"

I started to panic. I had not anticipated being asked who ordered Ruth away. I couldn't possibly say Missus Edith because word would get back to her, and if their plan didn't work, I had nowhere to go.

"Sir," Bill stepped forward, "Miss Anna has no knowledge of where the order came from, but she knows her father was very fond of the servant girl to the point that he left her in charge of Miss Anna."

The judge tutted, shaking his head. "You are right to assume this can be stopped, but there is not much I can do in the middle of the night. This will have to wait until morning."

"But, sir, she will be long gone by then," I protested.

He waved me away, turning back to his desk. "I can do nothing until the courts open. You – or better yet, your father, on his return – should approach me then."

I stood in the middle of the room desperately trying to think of something else to say that would change his mind, knowing each moment that passed Ruth got further away.

"Sir, I—"

I felt Bill's hand on my arm and he motioned me outside. The others jumped to their feet when we emerged from the house.

"Well?" Francis asked.

Bill and I shook our heads, and I was on the verge of tears because I had failed.

"He will not do anything until the courts open," Bill said, dejected. There was a sigh among all of them and they fell silent.

"I have to go after her," I choked. "I promised her I would find her. I have to go." The others looked to each other.

Francis approached me. "Who else knows about this?"

I wiped tears away with the back of my hand. "Everyone in the house."

"No one else?" he prompted.

I shook my head. "No, no one else."

The plan, Francis said, was to chase the carriage down. If we rode at full speed, we could catch them before they reached their destination. They weren't expecting to be followed and chances were the ship they were intending to put Ruth on was another week away.

"They won't be in any hurry," Francis said. "They may even stop at some lodgings on the way."

"So, we chase after them," Albert said, "then what?"

"Then we bring her back," I answered, feeling almost hopeful.

"What they are doing is against the law," Bill added. "They may take it to the magistrate, but it is more than likely they won't."

Everyone nodded slowly as the plan sank in.

"Well?" Albert said, jumping into the driver's seat. "What are we waiting for? Let's go."

There was not much to see as the carriage sped out of London. Part of me wished I could see what was going on outside. I had realized quite quickly that the darkness terrified me if I couldn't see what was going on. I sat next to the window, Bella beside me. Across from me was Francis who was in deep conversation with Bill. Occasionally they glanced in my direction with what I could only describe as pity. I sighed, leaning my head against the wall of the carriage.

I was angry at myself for not being able to convince the judge. Ruth would have done it. Ruth could talk her way out of anything. She was rarely afraid, and even if she was, like that day at the plantation when the overseer wanted to whip her, she still stood her ground, because Ruth never faltered in what she believed in, even if it cost her.

I, on the other hand, had spent my entire life looking up to her. Her playfulness, her resilience, her strength. I had tried so many times to be like my sister but often when it came down to it, the only thing I could do was find someone stronger and braver than I was.

Usually, Mama or Papa.

I would never have thought of protecting someone the way Ruth did and that's why I loved her so much. Ruth showed me a better way to be. She taught me that even when she was afraid, she would still do what was right.

I had never felt like I was needed. No one really needed me for anything, not real things like solving problems or standing up for someone. For most of my life I wandered around the house, waiting for Ruth to finish her work, or helping so she would finish faster.

Sometimes my father wanted me to talk to ladies who had shown up without invitation and so I distracted them while he left out of the back door. But most of the time I was needed only to smile, nod, laugh in all the right places, say thank you, ma'am and sir. To play with their spoiled brats. I pretended to be like them so I could sit at the table and listen to their boring chatter, and uncomfortable conversations speaking about their slaves as though they were not human.

The wheel of the carriage bounced off what felt like a stone and it jolted us all forward, reminding me of where we were. I sank back into the carriage trying not to think about how scared Ruth must be. Even with all her bravery, I knew she must have been feeling so alone and afraid.

I thought back to when we had arrived at the house, and how Ruth had begged me to talk to Missus Edith but I had been afraid. Ruth thought I was afraid to lose my position but that wasn't it. I was afraid of upsetting Missus Edith when Papa wasn't around.

Without him, I had no voice. Missus Edith did not care that her brother was my father; all she cared about was that my mother was a slave.

It seemed the right thing to do, to keep our heads down and do as we were told for a quiet life. But maybe we should have found a way out of there before it came to this.

I sank further into the darkness of the carriage despite being thrown around by the uneven road outside. Bella had fallen asleep, her head flopped forward, her chin grazing her chest. Bill was reading a newspaper found in the carriage and Francis had closed his eyes.

I tried to sleep too but the night's events replayed in my mind, keeping me awake. I missed Mama. She always knew what to do. If she were here, she would never have allowed this to happen. But she wasn't here, so it was up to me to make it right.

Despite not thinking I would sleep, my eyes eventually became too heavy to keep open, and I fell asleep on Bella's shoulders only to be woken with a start what seemed like minutes later.

When I opened my eyes, the door of the carriage was open and the carriage was empty except Bella gently waking me.

"We are at a tavern," she explained. "It's the first one for miles. Albert thinks they may have stopped here."

Immediately, I was wide awake. I climbed out of the carriage, heart thundering in my chest. Albert, Bill and Francis were gathered against the shadow of the horse to avoid being seen. They beckoned me over and Francis explained everything. "This is where many travellers stop to eat and feed their horses. Maybe even stay the night. I suspect your sister will be taken to Liverpool, which is quite a journey and not one that they will undergo without a rest."

He led me by the arm to the head of the horse where we could see the tavern more clearly but still remained hidden.

From the outside, the tavern looked much bigger than the one in London. It was built of uneven stones, and yellow light streamed out of every window. It was hard to make out anything else in the dark but the stench of horse manure.

"The horses will be tied up around the back. But first you will need to go inside, Anna, to see if the men are there."

I lost my breath at the thought of going into that place alone. "Won't one of you come with me?"

Francis shook his head. "If any of us went in, it would arouse suspicion. It has to be you, Anna. Only you." He squeezed my arm reassuringly. "I have much faith in you; you are stronger than you think."

I was not so sure about that, but with some guidance from the others, I pulled the hood over my face and walked hesitantly towards the tavern. My legs began to shake and I was about to turn back when I felt someone beside me. It was Bella with a hood covering her face.

"I will wait for you by the door," she whispered as we reached the building. "If there is any trouble, scream my name as loud as you can." I glanced over at her, and I could barely make her out from the hood she was wearing.

I took a deep breath, placed my fingers around the door handle and opened it with one swift pull.

The buzz of chatter engulfed me and suddenly I felt so small and so afraid. Inside, the tavern was wide with low beams. Wooden posts were positioned in the middle of the room, forcing me to go around them while avoiding small wooden tables and men who looked rough around the edges with dirty hands and blackened clothes.

I sneaked a glance at each table, moving around them as if looking for somewhere to sit. A young girl in a tavern at this time of night didn't go unnoticed however, and I started to get strange looks. I grabbed the furthest table away from the door to avoid any suspicion. I sank away from the light, searching the room for the man who took my sister.

"What can I get ya?" A woman blocked my view, forcing me to look up. When our eyes met the woman frowned. "How old are you?"

I panicked, unable to speak. The woman repeated herself, this time leaning in closer as she said it. I leaned away, pulling my hood further over my face.

"I'm an orphan," I said. The woman straightened, observing me from under her eyelashes.

"You don't seem like an orphan," she said, nodding at my clothes.

I looked down at myself as if I had forgotten what I was wearing. I tried to think of something quickly. "You shouldn't be out here," the woman warned. "This is no place for you."

As she walked away, I realized half the room was

looking. I stood suddenly, rushing towards the door, knocking into a chair. "I'm so sorry," I apologized quickly, and that's when I saw him, sitting across from the chair I just walked into, bold as day, a piece of chicken in his hand, his mouth greasy from the food.

It was definitely him. How could I forget those arms as they carried my sister. That grouchy face and the snarl of his upper lip.

My mouth fell open and my feet were stuck to the ground. "What you staring at?" he barked. He turned to his companion, the woman who was waiting by the carriage outside Edith's house. "What's she staring at?"

The woman glared at me, then her expression changed. Her head tilted to one side. "Do I know you?"

I shook my head, pulling my hood further down. I stumbled through the room, bumping into tables, people telling me to watch where I was going until finally I flung open the door and rushed outside.

18.

ANNA

I stood in the doorway gasping for air, my chest so tight it felt like I might die any minute.

Someone pulled me into the darkness. It was Bella.

"What happened?" Bella asked worriedly, but I couldn't breathe. All I could do was point back inside the tavern.

"You saw them?" Francis asked, stepping forward.

I nodded, bending over and grabbing my knees.

"They saw me," I gasped. "They saw me."

Francis ordered Bella to take me back to the carriage. "Her sister must be around here somewhere," he said. "Most likely round the back."

Bella took my arm but I pulled away.

"It has to be me," I told them through gasps of breath. "I have to be the one to find her."

Francis laid a hand on me. "You have done enough, Anna. You are in no state to do anything else." I straightened my posture and swallowed down the fear.

"I'm all right now," I said, forcing a smile I knew would convince them. I never had to try hard to convince people I was happy. Just a smile, any smile. Mama said it lit up my face and drew people to me. It didn't matter that I was pretending. It didn't matter that I wasn't really happy. My smile was enough.

I never got to cry on Mama's shoulders like Ruth did, because when I tried, she always asked the same thing: "What do you have to be upset about, Anna?" so I learnt that I wasn't allowed to be sad, not looking the way I did. I was expected to be happy. Always happy.

"I'm not so sure," Bill said doubtfully, looking me over, and his words caught me off guard, but the others were already heading around the back of the tavern. I ran to catch up with them, pushing myself to the front beside Albert even though I had to run to keep up with him.

The ground was muddy and dark with only a small lantern that Albert had brought from the carriage to guide us. He spotted a building ahead.

Albert raised the lantern to see clearer. It was a barn, as

he suspected. "Where they keep the horses," he explained.

I could smell them before we even got close enough. The stench was overwhelming and I used the arm of my coat to cover my nose.

The barn had no doors and it was pitch black inside.

Albert tried to soothe the horses so they didn't alert everyone in the tavern. Meanwhile, the others separated to look for Ruth. I crept further to the left of the barn using the walls to guide me as I called out her name. It was frightening without Albert's lantern. I could barely see in front of my hands or where my feet were stepping.

"Ruth?" I called out desperately. What if she wasn't here? What if she was taken somewhere else and was long gone into the night? I felt sick and stopped for a second to let the nausea pass.

RUTH

It was the frightened horses that woke me out of my sleep. That, and the dog jumping to his feet and growling.

I listened, heart pounding, thinking it must be my kidnappers returning. The dog stood in front of me as if to protect me and we both waited for the inevitable.

Then a voice, calling my name. At first, I thought I must be dreaming and rubbed my eyes before listening again. The dog ran towards the voice, disappearing into the darkness, and now I really felt alone. Then I heard it again, that same voice, frantically calling my name.

Anna?

I climbed to my feet and squinted into the night. "Anna?" I said again, this time out loud, but with all the crying and screaming my voice was barely a whisper. I heard more voices then, and my sister's among them. "Anna!" I screamed. I heard her call for the lamp, and I could barely believe this was happening. Praying this was not a dream.

Then out of nowhere she appeared like an angel, a lantern held out before her and Francis beside her.

We both stared at each other in disbelief. "Anna?" I said again but this time it caught in my throat and I could barely hold myself together.

She ran towards me, throwing herself at me, and I sobbed into her shoulder as she wrapped her arms around me.

Someone untied my hands and I was able to wrap my arms around my sister. "You found me," was all I could say, and I was lost in shock and relief. To think my sister had found me when I had thought it was all over and I would never see her again was too much to bear. I cried uncontrollably.

Albert pulled us apart. "We have to go," he said

urgently. "The horses are making too much noise; we have to go now." I tried to stand but my legs gave way beneath me.

I looked up at Albert, frightened, "I can't."

He leaned down and scooped me up in his arms. He carried me out of the barn along with the others, Anna holding on to my hand for dear life.

She ran alongside Albert, not letting me go, and I chanced a look at her. Her face was focused, her eyes defiant. She was like a different person. This was not the Anna I knew. This was the Anna I had always wanted her to be, and this is what it had taken for her to find her strength. I squeezed her hand, but it was as if she didn't notice, she was so focused on getting me to safety.

We reached the tavern and hid behind the wall. Waiting, listening for any voices. "We're going to have to run," Francis whispered, pointing at a carriage waiting. To the right of us, I saw the dog that had kept me company. He watched, tail wagging, his tongue hanging out as if guarding us.

Albert held up his hand. He peered around the building, then nodded and beckoned everyone to follow as we made a run for it. As we ran out into the open, I heard my heart thumping in my ears. It muffled the sound of Albert breathing, and of our feet running through the mud.

I thought of all the things that could go wrong in this moment. How this could be taken away from me in a second if we were found out, and I willed Albert to go faster. As we reached the carriage, a boy I had never seen before, but seemed to be with us, said he would drive and climbed up to the box, grabbing the reins of the horse within seconds.

Albert carried me into the carriage and told my sister to sit next to me. We did not let go of each other as the others jumped in, just as the horse pulled off with a start before the door was even closed.

The driver pushed the horses as fast as they could go and we held on to anything we could inside the carriage to stop us being thrown from side to side. But no one complained and no one spoke. My head was pounding with fear as I begged the horses to go faster than they had ever gone so we could get as far away from here as possible.

I leaned out of the window and looked behind us, expecting to see that we had been followed, but there was no one. I leaned into the carriage whispering, "Faster, faster." I glanced around the carriage to see if anyone had heard me but I saw from everyone's eyes that we were all thinking the same.

It was an hour into the journey before Francis knocked on the roof ordering the driver to stop. I looked at him frantically. "But they'll find us," I said, "they'll know I've gone."

"We need a break," he said as the carriage came to a stop. "Just five minutes. It's been an eventful night."

Albert opened the door and stepped out. He stretched with a yawn as the others followed him out, cautiously glancing up and down the long empty road.

I was rooted to the spot despite Anna trying to coax me out. "Come on, Ruth," she said gently, "Francis says it will be all right."

I shook my head, refusing to move. "If dey see yuh, it's all right, but if dey see mi…" I shook my head again at the thought.

Anna moved to the seat opposite me, gently taking both my hands in hers. "You trust me, don't you?" she asked.

For the first time, I was the one cowering in the corner, terrified, and she was the one protecting me. She had saved me. I nodded and allowed her to lead me out of the carriage to where the others were waiting.

The first sign of daylight was upon us. The sky was grey with hints of blue, and we were surrounded by open fields. Bella brought out a blanket and a basket of food and it was welcomed as we all sat on the side of the road.

The others devoured the bread and cheese and hot tea in seconds while I kept a sharp look out, startling at every sound. Finally, once I was convinced we were not being followed, I took the drink Anna offered me and drank it gratefully.

"So, what now?" Bella asked us as we huddled together to keep warm. "Where will you go?"

Anna looked to me, but I had no answer. "We promised Mama we would stay together," Anna said, "and as long as we do that, nothing else matters."

I nodded in agreement, beaming with pride at my little sister.

"What about Martha?" Bill suggested. "She might take them in; she's always saying she needs the extra help."

Bella nodded, looking the girls over. "Yes, that might work. Can you sew?"

I nodded, relieved at the thought of not having to go back to Missus Edith. "Yes, I can sew."

"What can you do?" Bella asked Anna.

She thought about this for some time. " I think I can do whatever you teach me," she said, finally, causing the others to laugh. I slipped my fingers into hers and held on to her tightly.

"I will teach her," I said firmly. "She is a quick learner and you can rely on her. She won't let you down." Anna smiled a watery smile. "I'm so proud of you," I whispered so only she could hear.

When we first left Jamaica, I had no confidence she

could ever stand up for me. I thought I would be the one always fighting for her. When I was dragged out of that house last night, not once had I dared believe that my sister would find me. I should have believed in her. I should have known she would not let me go.

"Right," Francis said, standing; he flicked the grass stems off his suit. "Shall we go?"

We climbed into the carriage and Albert closed the door behind us. He leaned in through the window,

"Where to?" he teased. The others turn to us.

"To a new life," I shouted so the driver could hear me. Anna giggled and Albert banged the carriage door in celebration. He climbed up in front with the driver and shouted, "To a new life!" which made us all laugh, and one by one we took turns shouting as the carriage pulled off. Anna and I beamed and I knew she was thinking the same as me; so many possibilities lay around the corner.

Maybe Mama would be on the next visit with Master John. Maybe we could save enough money to go home and escape into the mountains.

Maybe this was the start of something new for us, but none of that mattered as long as we were together.

AUTHOR'S NOTE

About ten years ago, I came across the story of Ignatius Sancho. An African man who wrote a series of letters about his journey from slave to author, shop keeper and abolitionist in seventeenth century England. It was my first time learning about stories where we were more than slaves, and it took me on a fascinating and enlightening journey.

When I was asked to write for the Voices series, I knew it would be tough. As a Jamaican, our history is built on trauma and we have a lot of unresolved pain. But what I loved about this idea was telling stories about our existence in Britain way before Windrush. Stories that are rarely told, and I was excited to be a part of that.

I came across many stories, but two struck my interest. One was the story of Francis Barber, a young Jamaican who was brought to England and became Samuel Johnson's heir. If you haven't read about Francis, you should. It's a fascinating story.

The other story I came across that inspired me to write *Two Sisters* was a blog written by a man who was tracing the history of three sisters during the nineteenth century. All were slaves, one was mixed, and all of them at some point were separated, two ended up in England, and this was where the idea for *Two Sisters* formed.

It was important for me to not ignore the uncomfortable truth of how these girls would be treated. I didn't want to gloss over it but I also didn't want it to just be about their pain. I wanted to show them as people who had hope, who laughed and played, but more importantly I wanted their bond to be the forefront of the story. How it was always about their relationship and how despite their surroundings, despite their treatment, their bond was the one thing that got them through their story.

Though the story of Ruth and Anna is fictitious, there are facts within the story. Slave children were often taken from their parents and brought to England, where they were often paraded at parties as a sign of wealth.

The story of the tavern is true, black men and women would meet in this tavern and it would be an escape from their reality, and it was important for me to include that.

What I hope you get from Ruth and Anna's story is knowledge of the footprints Jamaicans had in this country way before Windrush. I hope it encourages you to delve deeper and find more stories about people like Ruth and Anna, Francis and Ignatius Sancho.